RYKER

A HOPE CITY NOVEL

KRIS MICHAELS

D1603622

WWW.KRISMICHAELSAUTHOR.COM

FAMILY TREE

The Cast of Hope City... so far:

Chauncey and Hannah King - Parents

King children in order of birth:

Brock

Brianna

Brody

Blayze

Bekki

Colm and Sharon McBride - Parents

McBride children in order of birth:

Sean

Kyle

Tara

Rory

Erin
Caitlyn

The vibration of his cell phone against the nightstand catapulted Captain Ryker Terrell from sleep. He narrowed his gaze at his digital display. *Son of a bitch.* Fifteen minutes of sleep. Maybe.

"What? What's wrong?" The soft, sleepy question came from the tangle of sheets beside him.

"Nothing, it's work. Go back to sleep." He grabbed the phone and slid his finger across the face.

"Terrell."

"Cap, this is Brody. We have a situation. Shit, actually, we have one hell of a mess. You might want to come out here."

He slid from the bed and watched as she

reached for his pillow and hugged it close. Fuck, he did not want to leave. Instead of settling back down into bed with her, he snatched his service weapon, badge, jeans, and shirt and slipped from the room, closing the door quietly. "Our people involved?"

"No sir, but the crime scene involves a case we're working."

That went without saying if his sergeant was waking his ass up at two in the morning. "What's the address?"

"798 Hyatt Place, Maple Hills."

"En route." He tugged on his clothes before he grabbed his service weapon and clipped it onto his belt then hooked his badge to the opposite side. With a swipe, he picked up the keys to his sedan and let himself out, locking the door behind him.

He cruised through the nearly deserted streets of Hope City and drove up to... a hell of a mess. His sergeant had pegged the situation, all right. Fire trucks and police vehicles lined the street.

"Well, hell." He parked and scanned the scorched vista. Visions of the debacle of a bust almost three months ago flashed through his mind. Another stately house gutted by fire. He exited the car and headed toward the crime scene tape. Brody

King noticed him and slapped the arm of his brother, Brock. They moved away from the small gathering of police and firemen.

"Captain." Brody acknowledged him as he approached.

"Brody." He responded to his sergeant and then glanced at Brock King. The homicide detective and he saw eye to eye as they were the same height, but he had a good forty pounds of muscle on the guy. "What do we have?" He nodded his head toward the shell of a structure beyond.

Brock motioned to what remained of the house. "Three dead bodies. It wouldn't surprise me if the brass forms an interdepartmental task force on this one. Homicide, suspected arson, and drugs. There was about a kilo of heroin found scattered throughout the kitchen, which was the only area the fire didn't gut."

Ryker crossed his arms over his chest and stared a hole into the decimated home. "IDs on the bodies?"

Brock shook his head. "No sir, the ME will have to use dental records for that. They're not recognizable. The fire made sure of that. The ME is on the way, I've done what I could until they process the bodies."

Brody kicked the ground and cleared his throat. "Cap, the house belongs to Paul Desoto."

He turned his gaze to his sergeant. "Damn lucky for that son of a bitch he's in jail."

Brody sighed. "No sir, he's not. When I got the call and Brock told me who owned the house, I called the Cascade just to make sure. The jailor on duty looked it up. He told me Desoto had a court appearance yesterday morning, the judge reversed his decision on no bail, and he was free by noon. I didn't get the notification. The jailor insisted— according to the paperwork—they made the notifications."

Ryker slid a pissed off glare to the house. "Who got the call?" If one of his people had failed to up-channel that shit, heads would roll.

"Colonel Fenton."

"Fuck." That *asswipe* Fenton.

"Yeah, after the bust with Clare Edelman, Fenton was acting JDET commander." *Because he'd relieved you of duty* wasn't said, but Ryker got the message, loud and clear. Brody shrugged. "This mess isn't on us."

"Bullshit. If I knew Desoto was out, I'd have had eyes on him. This," he motioned to the home left in rubble, "is on all of us because HCPD failed."

Brock shoved his hands in his pockets and cleared his throat. "Sir, from what Sean McBride was saying, the fire started at the back of the house. By the time someone—our people included —noticed it from the street, the men would have already been dead. You can't take this on, sir. Someone wanted the people in that house dead."

"McBride has the arson?"

"Yes sir." Brock nodded.

Ryker blinked and asked, "Wait, why are you working in Central District?" King worked in the Southern District.

Brock shrugged. "I transferred. The wife is still down south. Different offices but same hours. It works for us. She doesn't have me doing the caveman thing around her, and I don't have her hovering. And, before you ask, I requested the transfer after we took a long hard look at the situation. We need to be independent so we can work. Two strong-minded people. She's got a superb partner in Grant Couch and my partner will join me at Central when or if he ever comes back from his loan to the FBI. Until then, I'm breaking in new gold shields before they get their permanent assignment." He nodded toward the gathering of officers at the front of the building. One was in jeans and a t-shirt with his gold badge on one hip and a gun on the other.

Ryker rubbed the back of his neck and leveled his gaze on Brock. "Okay. I'll have my major call McBride's captain and yours. There is a strong possibility this directly results from the Peña Cartel eliminating witnesses." He motioned to the crime scene. "Mind if I look?"

"Not a problem. Follow me." Brock led the way through the crime scene tape that marked cleared areas for responding personnel. Brody fell in beside Ryker. They trailed behind Brock a bit. Brody quietly grumped, "Fucker should have told us."

"Should have, but you know he wouldn't." Especially if not telling Ryker would put egg on Joint Drug Enforcement Team's face. If he was anything, he was realistic. It had been just over three months since they had reinstated him after that dickhead Fenton had tossed him to the wolves. Cleared of any wrongdoing, he re-assumed responsibility as JDET Commander, then *Fenton* had received a reprimand for wasting the city's resources, which put Ryker's ass on a powder keg with Fenton waiting to light the fuse. The man was gunning for him.

The Commissioner had started the paperwork to remove JDET from Fenton's control and place it directly under Central Precinct's direct supervision, but the transition was taking forever. He understood. It took time to smooth feathers. The people over Fenton were not happy, and they were fighting the move. JDET made huge busts, they were multi-jurisdictional, and that meant it funneled federal money into the division. Only that money didn't make its way to JDET. No, Fenton kept the money the FBI and DEA sent and used it to beef up other sections under his control. That's why they'd done an end around the motherfucker and were now receiving a percentage of the monies forfeited from the massive drug busts they'd made. Fenton himself had threatened him —actually, the bastard flat out told him he would ruin his career. There were no witnesses to the conversation.

He stopped beside Brock King and shook his head.

"I'd prefer if we didn't get any closer, Captain. The crime scene techs and photographers are finished with the area for now, but we're waiting on the ME. When they're done, I'm going back in with the crime scene techs to see if the bodies were covering any evidence. Speaking of which..." Brock motioned behind them to the large black van that was arriving. "There they are. I'll go get them. Take your time."

As one, both he and Brody squatted down and peered at the dead bodies. The fire had made recognition impossible. Desoto could be any of the three, or he could be in the wind.

"Peña wants Desoto dead. The fire could have been Molotov cocktails again, like at the Edelmans'." Brody muttered the words.

Ryker nodded as he stared at the grotesquely twisted bodies, mouths opened in a charred scream. "It would appear Peña is cleaning house. We need to keep tabs on Clare Edelman. Find out what name they listed on her paperwork. If Fenton is on it, remove that fucker and put you, me, *and* Theron on that sheet. Also, get word to the US Marshals so they can inform whatever marshal has Edelman's husband's WitSec case to tell that man to be careful." Brody scribbled in his notebook as Ryker rattled off actions he wanted his sergeant to ensure happened. Ryker shifted and narrowed his eyes, scanning the area. "No way of telling if they died beforehand or died in the fire. Let's look at the kitchen."

They carefully retraced their path and headed to the side of the house. From the doorway, they surveyed the area. White powder covered the table. A scale, cellophane, and scrapers littered the tabletop.

"I had the crime scene techs do a drug test kit. This is heroin. I can't help but think someone interrupted the process of these guys cutting up and processing the H for sale."

Ryker nodded. "The question is why would Desoto be cutting heroin. He wasn't a dealer, nor was he a user."

Brody scratched his chin. "Think maybe he needed quick money and had some of this around as insurance?"

"Maybe." Ryker shook his head. "He could have been trying to get some quick money to make a run. Or someone was sitting on Desoto's place. Someone working for Peña. Desoto comes home, they hold him for the boss."

"Only the boss isn't in the mood to talk. He orders a hit and all three die." Brock's voice behind them finished the thought.

Ryker shot the detective a sideways glance. "That would be one of many theories."

"We can work through those ideas when I

receive the reports and evidence. Detective McBride is in the back. He's made the initial call of suspected arson, but he won't go further until he has all the I's dotted and T's crossed. He's talking to the fire chief. You might want to catch a word with him before he starts to collect his samples."

"Thanks." Ryker motioned to the drugs. "Brody, you have this. I'll talk to the arson investigator, then get going. I'm assuming someone responded with you?" His sergeant was a damn good detective, but he wasn't letting his people work alone after recent events.

"Yes, sir. I'm here with Patel. She's getting contact information on the people who reported the fire and is going over their statements. I wanted to know if they'd noticed any unusual traffic around the house lately." Brody's head swiveled until he found her. "There, with the older couple in bathrobes."

"Good. Brock, please keep us up to speed on your case. Brody, I'll see you at the office later." He left his sergeant and strolled around the building. The stench of burning materials—and yes, flesh—hung around the structure like a shroud. Sean McBride turned as Ryker approached. McBride's eyebrows flew up. Ryker got that a lot. Few captains made it a point to come to crime scenes, but JDET was a team, they *all* worked hard, and he wasn't a mouthpiece, he was a cop. Although of late, he'd been letting his new lieutenant take half the calls. Thank God Terrence Theron had taken over for Anderson. The man had experience with task forces and also had five years of SWAT under his belt. He was a hell of an asset and flowed into the team perfectly.

McBride snapped off his glove and extended his hand. "Captain."

Ryker shook the man's hand. "Detective. I understand you've determined this is an arson?"

"Initially, yes sir, that will be our call. Our impression is the fire may have started in this corner of the house. We've found patterns that would lead us to believe an accelerant started the fire here." He pointed to the far corner of the structure at a deeply charred area. "The glass in this location fell inward, as you can see by the lay of the shards here and here. Normally, when fire causes windows to blow, the shards will be immediately under the casing or, to a degree, in an outward arc. There are several shards of broken, melted, colored glass throughout this room, which would lead me to believe the accelerant was in glass containers. I suspect the fire spread from points too because of the extreme speed with which the house burned. We don't know what accelerants they used. Once the fire chief has declared the scene safe, my partner and I will climb in and get to work."

"Sounds good. Someone will contact your captain. I'd like a copy of the reports and any information you find as soon as you validate it through the lab. Of course, wait until your captain tells you that."

McBride chuckled. "Wouldn't dream of jumping the gun, sir."

"I'll get out of your hair. Good night."

McBride glanced at his watch. "It's almost three. Don't you mean good morning?"

Ryker shook his head. "No, I don't. I'm going home to take a shower to wash this smell off me and climb back into bed."

"Wow, can I get a job as a captain?"

He laughed. "Yeah, just keep putting in the crazy hours, study hard, and don't get dead."

"Don't get dead. Excellent advice." McBride saluted him and they both laughed.

He tipped his chin toward the remains of the

house. "Be careful in there. That thing doesn't look structurally sound."

"This one is better than some I've gone through, but I've got my hard hat and I've learned to have a very soft step."

"See, captain material." He raised a hand in farewell and headed back to his sedan. He palmed his cell phone and called his major.

"Hello."

"Hughes, its Ryker."

"Hold on." He could hear the man moving around and then the sound of a door opening and closing. "What's up?"

"They released Desoto from jail yesterday."

There was silence for a moment. "Why didn't you tell me yesterday, or hell, wait until morning? Why the 3 a.m. briefing?"

"We didn't know until we called the Cascade that they had released him. They notified Fenton. Not us."

"What? Why in the hell? Ryker, I'm not caffeinated. Spell it out for me, please."

"Desoto's house burned to the ground. King called the Cascade to make sure Desoto was safe. The judge reversed his no-bail order and Desoto was free by noon yesterday. The jail called the

JDET commander listed on the intake forms. Fenton."

"Oh, fuck..."

"Yeah, so now we have suspected arson, three dead. Unknown identities. About a kilo of H in the kitchen which looked like it was in the process of being cut."

"Wait, Desoto wasn't a dealer."

"Right."

"Peña. Shit. What do you need?"

"I need Fenton off my back and a coordinated effort with homicide and arson."

"You think this was a hit."

"I do."

"Oh, for fuck's sake, just what this city needs, a drug lord on the warpath. All right. Look, I have to brief this up the chain. Fenton's my supervisor."

"Roger that. I'll be calling the Deputy Commissioner. At her request, I'm informing her of all incidents involving Fenton."

"I'll deny it if you tell anyone, but I'm so fucking thankful you have someone flying top cover that isn't under Fenton's thumb. That man has it out for you."

"Don't I know it." Ryker started his car. "I'll call you this afternoon if we have any updates."

"Are you heading into the office?"

"Nope. Home for a shower and some sack time."

There was a pause. "You feel okay?"

"Fine. I just need to get a few hours before I head to the office. I didn't get any sleep before they called me."

"Sleep in as long as you can. If anyone gives you shit, tell them I authorized it."

Ryker snorted. "If anyone gives me shit, they'll be eating their shoe."

Hughes laughed. "Yeah, true. I forgot who I was talking to for a moment. I'll work that cooperation you asked for between the departments. I'm not telling Fenton about that. I don't need him trying to block communication on this one. Call me when you have an update."

"Copy. Night." He ended the call and sighed. Hughes was a damn good cop, and he'd make a fantastic colonel. Unfortunately, Fenton was a weasel and it would take a stick of dynamite and a crowbar to remove the guy from his current position. So, the rest of the organization suffered while the man acted like a tyrant. Thank God the Commissioner and just about everyone else was onto the asshole's games. He thumbed his contacts and found the number for the Deputy Commissioner. The call lasted two minutes, but it was two minutes well spent. If Fenton could spin tonight's events to cast a shadow on Ryker or his team, he would. Letting the Deputy Commissioner know what had transpired before Fenton could throw it in his face took a ton of pressure off his shoulders.

He drove up to his small Craftsman, turned in the driveway, and parked beside the old SUV. Letting himself inside, he locked the door behind him, stripped away the foul-smelling clothes, and put them directly into the washing machine. Quickly loaded with soap and two caps full of those good-smelling beads, he prayed the stench of the fire would come out on the first wash. He liked those jeans, and the t-shirt had been a gift.

The selector button slid to heavy wash with a flick of his thumb and he depressed the button, starting the machine. With a soft click, he shut the laundry room door behind him and padded straight into the bathroom. His little house had two bedrooms and one bathroom. It was functional and worked for him. Small enough to keep clean and big enough to have everything he needed. He showered quickly, scrubbing hard to get the smell of smoke off his body. Unfortunately, the stench seemed to be pasted inside his nose. He gave up after the third round of suds and shampoo.

Drying off first, he brushed his teeth and headed to bed. He slid in between the sheets and gathered the warm, soft body sleeping on his pillow closer.

Brianna King sighed and then purred as she cuddled next to him. "Back from work?"

Her soft question tugged up the corners of his mouth. "I am."

"Are you okay?" Her hand skimmed upward and landed against his pec, over his heart.

"I'm okay. Go back to sleep."

She hummed. "What time is it?"

"After four, I guess."

"What time do you have to be at work?" She leaned away. Her beautiful blue eyes, heavy with sleep, stared up at him.

"When I get there." He turned on his side so they were face to face.

Her fingertips trailed over his chest. "So, you could sleep in with me?"

"I could." A smile formed on his lips as she leaned in and kissed his chest before she slipped further, trailing her lips across his abs and still down further. He rolled onto his back and moved his legs apart, giving her room. His hands found purchase in her long dark brown curls and held on gently as she circled the head of his cock with her tongue. Her hands cupped his balls, and she sucked him into her mouth. Fuck, the woman somehow knew what he needed. She hummed around his cock, wetting it before she took him farther into her throat.

"God, babe." He strained against the need building inside him. She was fucking talented. Her tongue worked his shaft and the suction, oh, damn, the suction and fondling of his balls had him pegged in no time. She pushed down; the head of his cock slid into her throat. She gagged but repeated the move again and again. The tight grip of her throat and warmth of her mouth were too much. He tugged her hair, letting her know he was close. She moaned and once again impaled herself on his cock, taking him to the back of her throat.

He curled up as he came. His fist tightened in her hair, and his cock flooded her mouth with his release. Her tongue lapped and swirled as she drank down all he gave her. He flopped back onto the bed and shivered when her tongue danced over his spent cock. Hypersensitive, he hissed. She pulled off and crawled up his body before she laid on top of him. "Welcome home."

"Damn, I'll ensure I get called out every night." He pushed her curls away from her face and brought her down for a kiss. "I'll return the favor. Just give me a minute to catch my breath."

"No need. You took excellent care of me earlier." She dropped to his side and tugged up the blanket which had slipped to his knees. "Any of your people hurt?"

He shook his head. "No. Although, I spoke with Brody and Brock."

"Mood gone." She groaned and flopped onto her back. "How did I let myself fall for the JDET Captain?"

"Well, to start with, I didn't tell you what organization I was with, just that I worked in Public Relations. I wasn't the commander of JDET... because of the circumstances."

She snapped her head back toward him. "Yeah, that's right. It's your fault. No, wait, it's that asshole Fenton's fault."

He laughed and brought her closer. "That's right, you can blame it all on him."

"Damn straight." She swirled her finger across the hair on his chest. "Mom is still angling to meet you. I keep putting her off. Thank God she has Gage to keep her occupied."

"I have no problem meeting your parents." He ran his hands through her hair. His eyes closed as he held her, and he yawned until his body shook. God, he wasn't twenty-something any longer. He needed to get some sleep at night. Working through the night didn't used to be a problem. Now? Well, he was keeping late nights waiting for Brie to close the restaurant and make it to his house. He'd happily drink more coffee to stay awake during the day so he could spend his nights making Brianna happy.

"See, you really don't know what you're getting yourself into. My brothers are horrid. You don't know them away from the job. My dad isn't much better, especially when he gets with Colm."

He had to think for a moment and then remembered. "The neighbor."

"Closer than neighbors. The McBrides are family."

"I can handle it." He yawned again.

"See, that's just it. I don't want you to *have* to handle it. Why couldn't I have a normal family?"

He chuckled and moved, situating her on his

bicep and getting comfortable. "You have a normal family. A regular Norman Rockwell painting."

"What about me meeting your family?" She snuggled closer and slid her leg across his. He loved the way she wrapped around him.

"Not the same as your family. No Christmas card moments there, but I'll introduce you to them if you'd like."

"Maybe we should just be happy with each other for a while longer first?" She placed a kiss on his chest, and he smiled with his eyes closed.

"Whenever you want, babe. Until then, my lips remain sealed." He drew a deep breath and let it go slowly.

"Thank you," Her whispered words against his chest were the last thing he heard before he drifted to sleep.

CHAPTER 2

Brianna drove down Jefferson and frowned. A police car was double-parked in front of her restaurant. No... they were in front of the small shop next door. She slowed to a crawl and craned her neck to see what was happening. Mrs. Paradelle was motioning to the broken storefront window. *Ouch.* That would cost a pretty penny to replace, especially if Mrs. P. didn't carry good insurance.

She sped up and went around the block, turning into the alley behind the restaurant. There were four parking spaces reserved in the rear for her restaurant. One for her, one for the front of house manager, one for the chef, and one for deliveries. Her staff parked farther down in the large parking lot at the end of the block. She paid their parking fees as part of their compensation package. Small things made a big difference to her staff, and she hadn't lost an employee in two years. They were happy, she made a decent income, so it was a win-win for everyone.

She drove her old SUV into her slot, locked it, and headed into her pride and joy. *Horizon.* The establishment she'd turned around—with a little help from her cousin, Justin. The man had a Midas touch, and when the restaurant came onto the market, she'd asked for his advice. He was so generous that he and his wife Dani flew in from New York and did a walkthrough of the property. He rattled off countless suggestions, and Dani had done a survey on the location, deeming it in a great central placement with future growth potential. With solid advice from Justin and Dani King, she purchased the place and slowly implemented the changes he'd recommended. Mortgaged to the moon, turning a real profit had taken years, and because she'd invested her profits without paying herself as much as she paid the chef or the manager of the front of the house, she'd lived frugally.

She unlocked the back door and let herself in,

turning off the alarm after she locked herself inside the building. Her office was off the kitchen, away from the public spaces. She flipped on the light to her tiny space and turned on her computer. She'd already dropped the cash deposit from last night in the nighttime drop box for her bank on her way to Ryker's, but she still needed to do her accounting, go through the orders, and pay vendors. There was always something to do.

The restaurant came to life shortly after she entered her office. She could hear the kitchen staff laughing and the clang and clink of pots, pans, and utensils being used. Garlic and onion and the smell of roasting beef reminded her tonight's special was prime rib. She needed to tell the chef to save her two servings. They usually sold out before the restaurant closed. Ryker loved it, and they'd had several late, late dinners at his house or hers. Her phone rang, and she glanced at the face before rolling her eyes. Her mom. She picked it up and put it on speaker. "Hi, Momma. I'm not late calling, I told you I was calling at ten." She glanced at the clock. She still had twenty minutes.

"I know, but I need to pop over to Gage's school. This week is the big book fair, and I volunteered to work it. I wasn't sure if I'd told you. I didn't want you to think I'd ducked your call." Hannah King laughed.

The lighthearted sound made her smile. "You forgot, but it's not a problem. Why don't we do lunch next week after the book fair is done? We can visit and catch up."

Hannah squeaked, "On clam chowder day?"

She laughed at her mom. "Yes, and bring Sharon with you. Chef has a recipe for sourdough bread that is fabulous with a salted herb butter he's created. It is divine."

"That sounds wonderful. I want to hear all the details about your new beau. I know you wanted time to spend with him, but it's been a long time. Perhaps we can schedule a dinner at the house?"

"Mom, this is the first genuine relationship I've had. I like this guy and I don't want the boys pulling their puffed-up caveman routine. And Daddy... he will grill him."

"Your father has grilled none of your boyfriends." Hannah tsked and continued. "I can talk to the boys. They'll behave."

"Maybe we can talk about scheduling a dinner next week at lunch?"

"That wasn't a no." Her mother pointed the obvious out.

"To be honest, Mom, he's said he doesn't have a problem meeting you. It's me. I don't want to jinx this."

"Brianna Marie King, your family is not a jinx!"

"No, I didn't mean it that way. I am just afraid of pushing it too fast, of doing something that will break this wonderful bubble we have surrounding this relationship. He's so good to me, Mom. I'm terrified of screwing it up." She stared at her desk blotter, not really seeing it.

"Honey, if this man is right for you, having him meet us will not screw it up. If your brothers trying to protect you chases him away, maybe he's not strong enough to be there for you."

"Mom, the boys would never run him off, it's the fact that they'll be assholes on purpose."

"Language."

She rolled her eyes at her mother's caution. "Mom, he's an amazing man."

"Then let us meet him, honey. I promise to put the boys on notice."

"And the McBrides, too."

"I'll talk to Sharon. We still can snatch those young men by the ear and twist if we need to do it."

She chuckled at the thought of her mom grabbing Brock or Brody's ear. Blayze—that she could picture. "Okay, we'll set a date next week at lunch."

"That sounds perfect." Hannah sighed. "Brie, honey, I'm so happy we've gotten closer and can visit about things like this."

She closed her eyes and smiled. "We were close before, Mom, but you were pushing so hard to find me someone, I'll admit I was trying to avoid all contact. It wasn't exactly comfortable."

"I know. I promised myself I'd try to do better." Hannah laughed. "No more helicopter mom."

"Hover Mother." Brie laughed at Hannah's sound of derision.

"I've got to run. Have a wonderful day."

"Thanks, Mom. Have fun at the book fair."

She disconnected the call and leaned back in her chair, a faint smile lingering on her face. "Hey, Boss. Did you hear what happened to Mrs. P.'s place?" Lola, her hostess and front of house manager, stood at her door.

Brie shook her head. "No, when I came to work this morning, I saw a patrol car there, but I didn't stop."

"Mrs. P. was outside sweeping up when I walked by. Some asshole threw a brick through her plate-glass window."

"Why would anyone do that? It's a small travel agency. Someone mad at a bad cruise booking?"

"No. She's really upset though." Lola leaned against the door frame. "Scary."

"That's so sad. Hey, put a to-go order in for her and have someone take it to her before we open."

Lola smiled. "I figured you'd want to do that. I already talked to the chef. If you didn't mention it, I would pick up the tab."

"Nonsense. We take care of our neighbors. Oh, speaking of which, if Councilman Davis comes in, let me know."

Lola nodded. "Sure will. Are they still stalling the ordinance change?"

"Unfortunately, yes. I gave them the petition with the signatures, we've done the yearly cost breakout for the delivery, even gotten insurance quotes and told them we would not hold the city responsible, would fund the program, and would sign waivers, but somehow it keeps getting pushed to the side for more urgent business. I hate wasting food."

"I'll keep my eyes open." She glanced at her watch. "I better get up to the front, we open in twenty minutes. Oh, Jeremy is running late. His babysitter called in sick, so he's scrambling to find someone."

"Do we have enough servers without him?"

Lola shrugged. "We could get by if need be, and I could bus when I don't have to work the stand."

"No, I'll bus the tables. Move Parker to cover Jeremy's tables, he's done it a couple times, and although he doesn't like it, he's competent. Tell Mark I need him to keep the front of the house running and you need to stay at the hostess station. Also, please call Jeremy and tell him he's got the day off with pay. Hopefully, he'll be able to find alternate care if the sitter is out longer than today."

Lola blinked and then shook her head. "You know, I don't think another boss in the city would bus tables for one of their servers, let alone give them the day off with pay."

Brianna frowned. "I'm sure there are many who would do the same thing."

"Boss, nobody has a heart as big as yours. We know we have it good here, and you got to know we are proud of what this place has become."

"It has been a team effort, that's for sure. Lord knows I didn't do this by myself." Brianna stood and stretched. "I'm going to change my shoes. I have a pair of flats in my SUV. Change the schedule and call Jeremy for me, okay?"

"Got it."

She grabbed her keys and made her way through the kitchen. She snatched a baby carrot from Carol's cutting board. Carol's eyes got huge, and she spun. "Chef, Brianna's pinching food again."

She heard her chef's booming laugh throughout the kitchen. "She bought the food, she can eat it." Chef Roger Plummer turned away from the massive stovetop. "But not all of it, some goes to the customers."

Brianna stuck her tongue out at Carol. The woman laughed so hard she snorted and that set off the rest of the kitchen. Carol's laugh was contagious. Brie ate half of the baby carrot before she headed to the back door. She shoved the rest of the carrot in her mouth and concentrated on getting the key for her old SUV untangled from the keys for the restaurant. She managed it and popped the back door open. It only took a moment to grab the shoes and shut the door.

"You know who owns this place?"

Spinning, she gasped and backed up, slamming into the side of her SUV. "My God, you scared me."

An ugly smile spread across the man's face. His teeth were rotted and grey, which matched the pallor of his skin. Thick, ratty blonde hair fell in a snarl over his brow. He stepped closer, and another man stepped into view from the other side of her SUV.

"I asked you a question. You know who owns this place?"

The man's breath made her cringe and turn her head. "It would be best if you left now." Brianna nodded to the back door. "If I don't go back in there in the next minute, they'll come looking for me."

"That so?" He stepped closer and sneered.

Brianna straightened to her full height, realizing that the man was shorter than she was. With her shoes held to her chest, she stepped forward. The man's eyes widened for a moment, taken aback. "Why do you want to know?"

The other man moved closer. The talker, emboldened by his backup, smiled.

"Hey Brie, phone call for you." Lola stood at the top of the stairs, the door held open. "You okay?"

"Ah, yeah. I'm fine."

The men drifted away from her and headed down the alley. Brie drew a deep breath. What a weird experience. She headed to where Lola waited. "Could you take a message? I need to use the bathroom and change." She held up her shoes and headed up the stairs.

"Sure, but it's Sexy Voice." Lola waggled her eyes.

Ryker. She chuckled and nodded. "Okay, yeah, I'll pick up in my office." She darted through the kitchen, barely cognizant of the people or the controlled chaos of lunch service prep. She closed her office door and drew a deep breath, and then another. She sat down and glanced at the phone, picking up the line Ryker used when she didn't answer her cell.

"Hello?"

"Hey, I forgot to tell you I bought tickets for us at the Capital Sunday night. They're showing *Chaos on the Crossroads*, you said you wanted to see it."

"Oh. That's wonderful. Okay." She fisted her hands to keep from shaking.

"Are you okay?"

"I'm fine. Just busy. We are down a waiter and I get to bus tables this afternoon." She cleared her throat. "I'd love to go to the Capital. I'll buy the popcorn."

"Nope, my date, the popcorn is on me. Hang on a second."

Brianna heard Brody's voice in the background telling Ryker they were ready to brief. "All right, give me five minutes. Have everyone involved in conference room one and make sure Lieutenant Theron is there, too."

"Sounds like you're busy, too." Brie drew another breath in and let it out slowly. The shakes had abated some.

"Unbelievably busy."

"A continuing case?" She unclenched her hand and sat the shoes down on the floor, slipping off her boots.

"Yeah. Peña. Again."

"That means it will involve Fenton. I'm so sorry. Is there anything I can do to help?"

There was a long, tired sigh. "Come to my house tonight? Things are better with you in my arms. I forget the darkness of my job when you're with me."

She closed her eyes. He dealt with so much. She could remember her father coming home, drained and just standing, holding her mom. What these men and women dealt with daily would wreck lesser people. She smiled as she spoke, "I'll be there. I like to snuggle in your arms. I'll bring dinner and wine and we'll curl up in your corner on the couch."

"Good. That thought will keep me sane until tonight."

"Please be careful. I'll see you tonight." She hung up and closed her eyes. God, the thought of him holding her made her feel safe. She shook her head. When had she become *that* woman? The one that needed a man to protect her? She'd never let a man take care of her, but Ryker was different. He was strong but let her be her own woman. They were on equal footing, both successful and both career-minded. They just fit together. She wasn't joking when she told her mother it terrified her the bubble would burst.

Those two assholes in the alley had really spooked her. Maybe that was why she was thinking about how safe she felt with Ryker. She ran her hands through her hair. Her brothers would have a field day with her getting a fright from two lowlifes. Her brothers' alpha male, *'me have club, me protect'* mentality got old quickly. She'd taken self-defense classes and could protect herself. She even had a concealed carry permit. At her father's insistence, she'd learned how to handle, care for, and shoot a weapon. He'd wanted her to have protection when dropping off night deposits after the restaurant closed. Not that she routinely carried her gun, but she could if she ever felt the need. A chill went down her spine at the thought of that man's sneer. Perhaps she'd take a half-hour this afternoon and pop home, grab some clean clothes for tomorrow, and take her gun from the lockbox. If she had time.

Lunch service was always insane. The constant influx of new diners kept her running, and she once again learned to appreciate what her people did daily. "Boss, Councilman Davis is at table fourteen, he's almost done eating. I'm sorry I forgot to tell you when he came in." Lola darted back to the hostess stand. Brie finished bussing two tables before she stashed her bin and table cleaner. A quick hand wash and she was threading her way through the seating area.

"Councilman. Nice of you to join us today." She stood beside his table and smiled at him.

"Short on help today, Ms. King?"

"One of my waiters is out today. Childcare issues. May I?" She pointed to the vacant chair across from him.

"The apron is a pleasant touch." He nodded to the chair.

She glanced down and shrugged. It wasn't dirty. She pulled the chair out and smiled. "Have you heard of anything about the ordinance change?"

The man took his time buttering a baguette. "Things like this take time, Ms. King. Greasing wheels and changing minds."

She blinked at him. "This ordinance change is for the good of the city."

He took a bite of his bread and settled back against his seat. After he finished what was in his mouth, he took a drink. She narrowed her eyes at him. The bastard was making her wait. Finally, he cleared his throat and spoke slowly as if she was three years old, "Ms. King, I regret to inform you that not everyone is in favor of changing the ordinance. There are many who do not want the homeless population catered to as it could draw more vagrants to our city."

"What?" She couldn't believe what she just heard.

"It is a simple truth. However, there are ways to make things go easier, to convince those who don't approve." He shrugged and stared through the large front window.

"What do I need to do to get this changed? I'm throwing away food every night. Food that could feed people. I'm not asking to open a casino."

Councilman Davis smiled; well, rather, he smirked. "No, I'm sure you'd have less difficulty with that." He turned to face her. "Money talks."

She leaned in, "Are you asking me for money to push this through?"

"That would be unethical." He stared at her. "What I am telling you is that your ordinance is not on the docket for the next meeting. I don't think there are any other motions to discuss. Such a shame, but as I said, money talks." He wiped his mouth and placed his cloth napkin down on the tablecloth. "Once again, lunch has been wonderful. Thank you." He stood up, adjusted his cuffs and jacket, and walked out of the restaurant.

"Hey, is he leaving?" Skip, one of her full-time servers, stood with a payment folder in his hand.

"He is. Why?" She stood up and started stacking the man's plates.

"He didn't pay." Skip blinked at her and looked at the padded folder in his hand.

She stood up and stared after the man. He stopped at the door and gave her a small salute before he walked out of the door. *Well, son of a bitch.* "His meal today is on the house." *Obviously.* "Include your tip on the receipt."

"Are you sure?" Skip looked from the door to the folder.

"You deserve payment for your time." She grabbed the asshole's stack of dirty dishes and headed to the back of the establishment. What was she going to do now? Would he stop the ordinance change? They could feed hundreds of people a day. Thousands of meals throughout the year. She put the dishes down and headed to the front with a bin and her cleaning supplies. Thoughts raced through her mind until only one remained. *How much money was the man talking about?*

CHAPTER 3

Ryker watched his people filter from the conference room until only three remained. He leaned back in his chair and looked from Brody King to Terry Theron. "So, any updates from last night?"

"I received a call from Captain Jones while you were on the phone earlier. He indicated that both McBride and his partner Miller returned from taking samples and going through the scene during the daylight hours. No doubt about it, they are calling it arson." Terrence leaned forward, his elbows planted on the conference room table. The veins under his rich brown skin popped vividly against his muscles. The man had about zero percent body fat and was a dedicated lifter like

Ryker. Terrence had won a couple of regional bodybuilding championships. The stacked guy was about the nicest man on the planet—unless you were a scumbag or a suspect, then he was hell on wheels. Ryker had known him in passing for years, and he'd always liked the guy. He was damn glad to have him on the team.

"Figured as much." Brody took a drink of his coffee.

"Autopsies scheduled for tomorrow?" He grabbed his mug and swirled the dregs of his second cup of coffee. The oil on top warned him not to drink it, but fuck it, he needed a boost. He downed the sludge and grimaced. "Who the fuck made the coffee?"

"I have no idea who made it, but it is nasty." Brody yawned and launched his paper cup toward the wastebasket. "I called and verified the victims were on slate for examination tomorrow. Brock collected the heroin and logged it into evidence." Brody yawned again. His entire body shook.

He glanced at Terry. His lieutenant gave him a slight nod. "King, you and Patel get your ass out of here and grab some sleep. Did you drive in with your wife?"

"Nah, we brought two cars. We usually do in

case one of us gets stuck late, the other can pick up Gage." Brody stood and stretched. "I think I'm too old for this shit, Boss."

Ryker rubbed his eyes. "That makes two of us." He yawned at the same time as Brody.

Terry chuckled. "Single men like me don't have that problem. At least not on weeknights. Weekends, I'm wrecked."

Brody dropped his hands and frowned. "You got a woman, Cap?"

Terry's eyes widened when Ryker sent him a side-eyed glare. Terry cringed. "Shit, I just assumed everyone knew. Sorry, man."

Brody raised both hands. "No worries. I can keep a secret. Glad you found someone. You'll have to bring her to the next barbeque so we can meet her. Bet she's one hell of a lady."

"Has to be to keep this old dog from sniffing around." Terry slapped him on the shoulder.

Ryker didn't need that type of talk around Brianna's brother. He closed his eyes and shook his head. He needed to stop this shit in its tracks. "My personal life, as always, is not up for discussion."

"What about for trashing?" Terry laughed and ducked at the glare he sent his direction. He held up his hands. "All right, I give."

"King, get your ass out of here. Terry, we need to review the cases that will go to court soon and work the schedule to make sure we have the officers involved available."

Terry snared his tablet and King waved, yawning again, shuffling through the door. His sergeant shut the door behind him. He leveled a stare at his old friend and lieutenant. "Drop the talk about my lady."

"Dude, I was joking. No offense meant. I'm sure she's a wonderful woman." Terry's eyes held honest regret.

He glanced at the door and then back to Terry. "Between us and absolutely no one else?"

"You know I can keep a confidence. I just assumed everyone knew you had a lady. I overheard you talking to her a couple times."

"Yeah, well, my woman is Brody and Brock's sister."

Terry stared at him for a long moment before a wide smile spread across his face. "You dog! You're robbing the cradle!"

He groaned and dropped his head back on the chair. "She hasn't introduced me to the family yet. Can't say as I'm looking forward to the fallout, but she's worth it."

Terry clamped a hand over his mouth and laughed, "Oh, fuck! You're dating the commissioner's daughter! Fenton will have a brain hemorrhage!"

He snorted. "Yeah, well, he will shit a brick when I ask her to marry me."

Terry's laughter stalled. "How long have you been dating?"

"Almost three months."

"Kinda fast there, isn't it?"

He shook his head. "Not for me. I'm turning 47 this year, I've run the race, and I can tell you no one has ever been better for me than this woman. She's strong, independent, knows a cop's life, and she's got her own life together."

Terry stared at him and then narrowed his eyes. "Yeah, that's fine, but do you love her?"

Ryker leaned forward and stared into the bottom of his coffee cup. "I'm in deep. Yeah, I do."

Terry reached out and cuffed him on the arm. "Yeah, but does she know?"

Ryker chuckled. "I haven't said the words, but I think she knows."

Terry looked at him and shook his head.

"What?"

"My mom, you've met her, right?"

"Yes, I have. She's amazing." A take-no-shit-from-anyone kind of amazing with a stare that could make you feel you were ten years old.

"Yeah, that's one word for her. Anyway, my mom taught me two things about women. The first, never assume a woman can read your mind. She can't and, not only that, evidently, according to what my momma drilled into me, she doesn't want to."

Ryker chuckled. "Ah, huh. Noted. What's the second rule?"

"A lady is always right, even when she isn't." Terry arched a single eyebrow. "Didn't your momma ever tell you these things?"

Ryker huffed and shook his head. "My mother was busy raising four other boys. I got my education through the school of hard knocks."

"Oh, don't you think my momma didn't knock me around. She did. I still have a bruise on my ass from the last whipping I got with that wooden spoon."

Ryker burst out laughing. "Yeah, when was that?"

"I'm thirty-nine, so thirty years ago." Terry's laughter melded with his.

"I see the captain and lieutenant of my Joint Drug Enforcement Team are hard at work."

Ryker turned his attention toward the door. The mirth of the moment dried into nothing. "Colonel Fenton." He and Terry stood. "How may I be of assistance?"

"You can explain to me how Desoto died." The man's face was beet red and a vein bulged on his large, bald head.

"As of this moment, we are uncertain Desoto is dead, sir." He crossed his arms and waited.

Fenton blinked and his mouth fell open before he snapped it shut. "I received notification that his house burned down and he and two others were dead."

"You did? From who? I know the reports we sent forward were that we had three unidentifiable bodies and pending forensic identification they would be John Doe one, two, and three."

"It was your responsibility to bring the Edelman case to court. With Desoto dead, you have nothing."

"Not exactly accurate either, sir," he interjected. "We have the Edelmans' testimony, video of the events of the night, physical evidence in the form of letters Desoto wrote to Clare Edelman, and the crates of pressed Gray Death that we removed from her greenhouse. The DA believes we can still go forward with the case."

"There is no way to pin this to Peña without Desoto's testimony."

"I believe the DA is aware of that, too." Cliff Sands was trying to get Clare Edelman to roll on Rubio, which would put them one step closer to Peña. He wasn't sure if his superior had any idea about the connection between Rubio, Desoto, and Clare Edelman, and he would not put that information in front of his glory-mongering boss.

"This team is a miscreant-filled mess. Your mismanagement of the Edelman case borders on criminal. I'm watching you, Terrell. You breathe in the wrong direction and I'll dismantle this team. You may have friends in high places, but mine are higher."

Ryker arched an eyebrow. Fenton wasn't the only one who could throw out threats. "Yes sir, and sir, may I ask why you didn't inform anyone that Desoto made bail yesterday?"

The man squared his shoulders. "Are you suggesting I failed to pass on information that would have prevented the events of last night?"

Ryker stood his ground with Terrence right

beside him. "No sir, I asked why the information didn't come to us."

"I didn't receive any information about Desoto until Major Dewitt contacted me last night to inform me of yet another fiasco."

"My detectives must have misunderstood what the Deputy told them."

Fenton sneered. "*That* seems to be the standard for this team. I'm watching closely, Captain."

"Duly noted, sir."

The man spun on his heel and stomped out of the room. Terrence released a huff of air, his shoulders lowering a bit. "Motherfucker is a snake."

"He is. Get with King. I need the name of the jailor he spoke with, and I need a copy of the paperwork showing Fenton received the notification. Make it happen before Fenton can cover his tracks."

"On it, and Ryker, don't let this guy get to you. The commissioner has your back and every person out there would go to the mat for you." Terry dropped a heavy hand on his shoulder before he power-walked from the conference room. Ryker dropped into the chair and drew a deep breath while he stared at the fake wood grain of the table.

It was one thing for Fenton to be gunning for him, but the people on his team were outstanding. When the asshole called them miscreants, a red flag had waved in front of his eyes. He should have said nothing. He should have taken the verbal barb and let it wash over him like the rest of the shit Fenton said, but damn it, he would not let that man take aim at his team.

He leaned back in his chair and stared up at the clock. There were options. Options he didn't want to think about, but if push came to shove and his people were in Fenton's direct line of fire, he could punch out. An early retirement would remove Fenton's bullseye from the team. He could find work somewhere. He had friends; hell, he could beg his half-brother for a temporary job. His gut rolled at that thought. Humbling himself to his half-brother would be a last resort. Fuck, retiring and giving up the fight would be the last thing he'd imagine happening, but after months and months of Fenton's accusations and attacks, it was a course of action he'd be smart to consider. A call to HR would start the rumor mills, but he could pull most of the documentation from HR's website.

"Cap, Rayburn and Watson just brought in

Mouse." Patel's voice from the doorway snapped him from his defeatist thoughts.

"Copy that. What interview room is she in?"

"Three. She's tweaking a bit, but coherent."

"I'll be right there." He stood up and squared his shoulders. Fenton could push and threaten, but until there was something to worry about, he had a drug enforcement team to run. Drug dealers never stopped pumping poison into the city.

"Cap, I heard that jailor say they called Fenton. Sergeant King had the phone on speaker. He read it right off the form. I know the jailor, too. He's straight up and isn't on the take. If that paperwork disappears, he'll make a statement as to what he saw. We got your back."

He smiled at Patel and nodded. "Thank you, but you shouldn't have to worry about me, you have enough to worry about doing your job."

"You watch out for family, Cap. This team is family. Kinda crazy, but family." They walked down the hall together.

"Don't you mean dysfunctional?"

"Nah, we function better than any other team on the force. Besides, you have to be a bit cray cray to work narcotics. We will never win the battle, but we keep charging up that hill." She peeled off to the left, and he headed right to his office.

He dropped his folders and his tablet on the desk before he made his way to interview room three. Mouse was his informant and about once every six months the woman would drop a text with an address. He'd send a team and pick her up. The girl traded information for a dry, safe 48 hours in the team's holding cell, nutritious food, hot showers, and a full bag of hygiene products when she left.

He opened the door and concealed a wince. Mouse looked bad. She'd lost so much weight her face was skeletal, and her bones punched through the thin shirt she was wearing. The kid was maybe twenty-four years old, and it didn't look like she'd see twenty-five.

He sat down. "Mouse. How you doing?"

"Not good." She held a bottle of water in her hands, which were noticeably shaking.

Ryker nodded. "What do you need?"

"Remember, a lifetime ago, you talked about rehab?" Mouse opened the bottle and used both hands to bring it to her lips.

"I do. I offered to get you into a program and I also told you I'd buy you a bus ticket back home once you completed it." He and Mouse went back about six years. She was fresh on the streets when he'd made that promise.

"If I had something really good... something that if I told you, it would get me ghosted. Could you send me to rehab out of the city and buy me that bus ticket?"

Ryker sat back in his chair. "I have little pull outside the city, Mouse, but I'd be willing to make some phone calls."

"No names!" Mouse's dark brown eyes shifted from the door to the two-way mirror.

"You have my word there isn't anyone behind that glass or outside that door listening. You're safe with me."

"Not if I talk. If I tell you what I know, I'm dead." Mouse coughed and put her water bottle down, wrapping her arms around her stomach.

"All right, say you had some intel, would you be willing to give a sworn statement to the DA in exchange for treatment and a ride home?"

Mouse sniffed and wiped at her nose. "Yeah, yeah, but no one could know where I was going." Her eyes darted around the room again.

"Have you told anyone where your childhood home is?"

"No. Nope. Never. Not a soul."

"Then how could anyone know? I'll go with you to the bus station, buy your ticket, and put you on that bus myself. You know I've never lied to you."

"Yeah. Yeah. Okay. Get the DA guy, but only him and you. Right?"

"Sure. Can you tell me what you have info on before I make that call?"

"Hit squad. Peña's hit squad."

"Everyone knows Peña's crew takes out people for him. You need to do better than that, Mouse."

"Yeah." Mouse's eyes traveled around the room again before she leaned in and whispered. "I saw Peña and Rubio with them. I was there when Peña told them who to kill."

"When?"

Mouse shrugged. "I don't know, the days and nights run together. They were in a warehouse, man. It was where I was crashing. I woke up and there were voices like right there. What they were saying, it was some serious shit. I could see Peña and Rubio."

"How do you know what Peña and Rubio look like?"

"Dude, everyone on the streets knows them."

"Mouse," he warned his informant. Broad statements like that would not cut it. He needed to know how his informant knew the kingpin and his second.

"Fine, I worked a party once; they were the hosts. Spent the entire night with them and their friends. They weren't particular about who they used as a hole. Believe me, I know who they are." She shrugged her shoulders and looked away.

Ryker held back the pity he felt for Mouse. Having to whore yourself to feed your habit was harsh. Life on the streets was a bitch.

"Anyway, I got a look at who else was there. I watched for five minutes or so. Heard everything. They told their guys to go to the burbs and follow a guy named Desoto, then kill the woman he met, but only after he got the last of the containers. Peña was bragging to Rubio that he'd figured out a different way to get the drugs in and couldn't have anything that would come back to them. I heard enough. I fucking ran, but not before I heard what they said and saw who was doing the talking. I've been hiding. Eating out of dumpsters and stealing to get my needs. I can't do it no more, man. They're hunting me. Peña and Rubio have a bounty on me."

"How do you know that?"

"Because Bingo tried to tie me up last night after we high-balled some H. Said with the money he would get by turning me in to them, he wouldn't be living on the street no more."

"How did you get free?"

"Fucker coasted on a highball. I ran while he was flying. Asked Alice to untie me and text that address to your number."

"How's Alice? Trustworthy?"

"She ain't a fan of Peña. She doesn't know whose number I gave her. She told me to leave town and not to come back, said if I didn't, I'd be dust."

"Where were you hiding?"

"Cardboard Cottages, some. Abandoned buildings past the harbor. Never anywhere long."

"How did Peña know it was you in the warehouse?"

Mouse stilled and examined her fingers. Finally, she spoke, "I had my stash there. Clothes, my winter coat, gloves. My name was in my clothes so if they got stolen I could prove they were mine."

"All right, Mouse. You hold tight here. I'll send you in some food and then my guys will take you to the cells. You can take a shower and sleep until I get this all sorted."

"Rehab, man? Out of the city? Not under my actual name. Peña's connected. If anyone could figure out who I really am, he could."

"I'll do my best."

Mouse whined, "Your best? Man, that could get me killed."

He shook his head. "I won't allow that to happen, but neither will I make promises I can't keep."

Mouse nodded and started rocking in the chair. "I got nowhere else to go. Try hard, yeah?"

"I guaren-fucking-tee it." He rose from the chair and headed to his office. On the way past the pen, he crooked his finger at Rayburn and Watson, who followed him. He motioned to the door and Watson shut it. "You've got a new assignment. Mouse is your new best friend. Get her food, shower, clothes, and put her in a cell here, not in city holding. One of you cut out now and come back for night shift. Don't leave her alone."

Rayburn arched his eyebrows. "She must have some serious 411 this time."

He nodded once. "Something that could blow shit apart for us."

"You've got it, Cap." Watson and Rayburn said the words at the same time.

"That was just fucking weird. Get out of here and you report to nobody but King, Theron, or me. Loose lips on this one will get people killed." The men hustled from the office, and he walked to his door. "Theron! King! My office."

Not a head in the bullpen turned his direction. They were used to his intercom system. Unless he bellowed their names, they kept working.

Terrence and Brody walked into the office and he once again nodded to the door, waiting for it to shut before he relayed the information Mouse had given him.

"I think Cliff would be very interested in this information." Brody leaned forward as he spoke. "I know we can trust Cliff, but I got to tell you, information comes from the DA's office when it is convenient for the DA. Is there a way to handle outside of HCDA's office?"

He nodded. "It was the hit ordered on Clare Edelman. We can tie it into the federal drug case. Federal prosecution."

"How are we going to avoid briefing Fenton?" Terrence asked. "We can't trust him to keep this to himself. He'll spout the information at a press conference to make himself look good."

"I'll brief the Deputy Commissioner and tell her of our concerns. She can make the call who gets a brief."

Brody rolled his shoulders. "I hate that we can't trust one of our own."

"The police force is a microcosm of our society. There're good and bad people on the force, even though we've done everything we can to weed out the bad seeds. Hell, ninety-nine percent of the people on this force would stand in the way of a bullet meant for someone they'd never met. The one percent who abuse the power of a shield are the ones that give us a terrible reputation. Fenton grew up during the old regime, the old days of give and take and deals made under the table. He's a product of his upbringing, but until he fucks up bad enough, he's still in our chain of command." Ryker eyed both of his... friends. "I and I alone will do anything that does not directly comply with department policy. Do we understand each other?"

Terry jolted in the chair he'd reclined in. "What the hell, Ryker? He's after you. If we do something out of bounds, he's not even going to notice." Brody nodded his agreement.

"That's where you're wrong. He tipped his hand this morning. He wants to dismantle this team and he'll take a shot at anyone to discredit us. No, I'll go to the Deputy Commissioner. They have directed me to take anything involving Fenton to her. She'll make the call. That way, we're all covered. Brody, as always, you do not have clearance to speak to your father about any of this without going through the chain of command, just like any other officer on any other case."

"I've never overstepped before, Cap. I won't start now." Brody shook his head. "Wish like fuck I could bend his ear, though. Fenton is a weasel."

"That's Colonel Weasel to you." A corner of his mouth twisted up when both men belted laughs.

"Watson and Rayburn are babysitting Mouse. Is the surveillance set up for the FBI's favor?"

Terry nodded. "Yeah, Brody and I just finished the roster. We have Cantrell and Lewis inbound. They said they got something from their CI."

He thought for a moment. "They're tracking the rumor of the cocaine shipments through the airport?"

"Yep. Mention of coke coming in via the airport has bubbled to the surface in three different interviews." Terry glanced at his watch. "They should be here in twenty minutes."

"Okay. You and Brody take this and run with it. Business as usual, except for Mouse detail. If anyone makes inquires, she's not here. I don't want to lose my best source of intel on the streets."

"That works. Nobody's going to ask, though. Not from this team, at least. We meet anyone asking about our shit with a stone wall. When we know our captain is being watched? Nobody is getting any intel." Brody stood and nodded to the door. "Want me to close this?"

"No. I'm going to Central and speak with the Deputy Commissioner in person." He grabbed his keys and followed his men from his office. He glanced at the clock and rolled his eyes. It was going to be a long fucking day.

CHAPTER 4

"I'm just about ready to get out of here. What about you?" Chef Roger peeked around the corner of the door.

Brianna glanced up from the deposit slip she was tallying. "I am. Hang on for just a minute and I'll walk with you." She glanced at the clock on her wall. "Why are you still here?"

He shrugged. "Tomorrow is chowder day."

"Ah, the sourdough bowls. Are they ready to go into the proofer? I can put them in the oven when I get here in the morning." She could slip in early and then go to the gym with Ryker before the day started.

"No, that's okay. We should be fine. Carol is coming in early to help me. The new fishmonger is dropping off our clams first thing. We are going to have a coffee and then get to shelling those clams."

"You know we could order them shelled."

"But why? It costs you more and we don't know how fresh they are. This way, I know my food is as fresh as possible." His bright green eyes flashed, and he smiled.

"You'd go harvest them yourself if you could, wouldn't you?"

"I would, and that is a perfect segue into this topic. What do you think about opening an organic, sustainable ingredient restaurant?" Roger leaned forward and placed his elbows on his knees.

Okay. That was one hell of a leap. "You realize that I'm just now turning a profit on this place, right?" She set her pen by the receipts she'd tallied.

"I do, but I also realize that this business was in very poor shape when you bought it. You not only had to rebuild it, you had to change people's perception about the establishment to bring the city back through those doors, and you've done that. We have a line out the door for lunch service and reservations for dinner are booked solid for almost three weeks. This place is about to make you rich."

She laughed, "And you want to put me in the poorhouse again."

"Not quite. I have a proposition for you. I'd like to go in fifty-fifty on the new place. I'd be the chef, take care of the kitchen, just like here. Together we hire the staff, manage the front of the house, and take care of the accounting."

She blinked as a chill went down her spine. "And where would that leave Horizon?"

"With me as the Executive Chef over both establishments. What we'd do is bring in a young chef who is hungry. One who wants to succeed. If he or she works out, we offer them this restaurant as executive chef and I push on with the organic place."

"You've been thinking about this for a while now, haven't you?"

"I have. I've watched the way you've run this place. You are a natural. You have zero staff turnover. Do you know how extraordinary that is? Most people cycle through waitstaff and kitchen help. Hell, most places need a revolving door to keep up with the flow of people in and out. But not you. You treat your people well, pay them well, give them benefits."

She nodded. The idea of another business set

her nerves on edge, but it was exciting, too. "I'll admit, I'm interested. I'd want to run it past my advisor, but after that, I'd be willing to take a hard look at what I can do."

"Advisor? You mean for finances?" Roger nodded. "Yeah, I can see that."

"No. Well, I mean yes. I'll have to get with my accountant and then the bank if we go forward, but Justin, my cousin. He's the one who advised me that this would be a wise investment, but it would take work. He's the one that pointed to you and told me I'd be a fool not to make you an offer."

"Justin King? As in the man with the Midas touch? The billionaire? He noticed me?"

She gaped at him. "He's not a billionaire."

"He must be." Roger nodded.

"No." She scoffed at him. There was no way Justin... no... "Can't be. He owns a few restaurants."

"A few? I guess if you consider at least six Michelin star restaurants around the world, franchises across the globe, and *owning* an entire building in the heart of New York City as the average Joe, then... yeah, okay."

She narrowed her eyes at him. "Are you playing me? How do you know that?"

He dropped his jaw and blinked. "How can you

not know this? He's been on the cover of every culinary periodical for the last decade."

"I don't know if we are talking about the same Justin King. My dad said he had a few successful places. I called him and he and his wife came up. We'd only met a couple times throughout the years. I told him I wasn't afraid of hard work, and that I wanted the place to succeed."

"Well, that's probably why he helped you. His work ethic is legendary."

"Huh. Okay, I'm still not convinced we're talking about the same guy, but anyway, I'm going to ask him what he thinks before I go forward."

"Can I meet him? I have a huge man-crush on the guy." Roger bounced in his chair and then laughed like a loon. "Justin-freaking-King!"

She shoved the money into the deposit pouch and laughed. "I'm telling you, you're thinking of a different guy."

"I don't think so. Big guy, good looking, black hair, green eyes, sexy as all get out."

She stopped what she was doing. "Just how much of a man-crush do you have?"

"Enough that I put him on my list."

"List?"

Roger cocked his head at her and pursed his

lips. "The list you and your spouse have? You know, if you ever do it with a celebrity, you get a free pass?"

What? "You *plan* on cheating on Matthew?"

"What? No! Every couple has a list. Ask your man. Bet he has one. Oh, and don't forget your prime rib dinners. They are in the cooler with a bottle of wine."

"Thank you, and I've never heard of this magical list. I think that may be a Roger and Matt thing."

"No honey, that's an *everybody* thing. You've led a sheltered life." They moved from the office and she turned off the light as they left.

She squared her shoulders and retorted with all the conviction of a three-year-old throwing a tantrum, "I have not." She stuffed the deposit into her purse and slung the strap over her shoulder.

"Mmm-hmm." Roger opened the cooler and produced two takeout boxes and a bottle of wine. He shoved the wine in her purse on top of the deposit and nodded to the door. He grabbed the containers. "I'll take these for you."

"Thanks, you go first and I'll set the alarm." He opened the door, and she keyed the alarm, quickly ducking out and shutting the door behind them.

She locked all three of the locks on the door and followed him down the stairs.

"Brie, you have a flat."

"What?" She stepped next to him and groaned. "I don't have a spare." She was supposed to get one... almost two years ago after a massive pothole on Millers Road devo'd her tire. "Damn it." She walked forward and bent down to look at the– "Aw man, who would do that?"

"What?" Roger leaned down. "Girl, someone *sliced* your tire!"

"It looks that way." The gash ran from the top of the tire down the sidewall.

"Come on, I'll drive you to the bank and then drop you off at Mr. Sexy Voice's house. You can call someone in the morning."

She stood up and sighed. "Thank you, but I can call an Uber."

"No, I insist. Matt won't be home for at least another hour. He closes the club tonight." He opened his car and put the prime rib in the back seat. "Come on."

She gave one more look at the flat tire before she sighed. "If you're sure."

"Positive. Now, let's get going."

Ryker leaned from his favorite position on the couch and stared through the picture window at a car that coasted to a stop in front of the house. Brie got out of the passenger seat, juggling two takeout containers and her purse. She laughed and waved at the driver. He opened the front door and watched her come up the walk. The driver waited until she made it to the door before they left.

He took the boxes from her. "Was that your chef? What happened to your SUV?"

"Yep, that was Roger. Oh, I should have introduced you, shouldn't I? Sorry, I didn't think to do that."

"No worries. What happened to your vehicle?"

"Oh. A tire that died, or rather, was murdered. Whatever happened, it is flat as a pancake." She groaned and dropped her purse on the small couch in the living room. "Hungry?" She kissed him quickly and headed into the kitchen with the wine.

He followed her and sat down the takeout containers. "Absolutely. Did you pick up a nail or something?"

She snorted. "Or something. Will you open that for us? I've had a weird day."

He opened the drawer with the wine opener and uncorked the bottle.

"Weird how?"

"Wow, okay. So, it starts with my mom, ends with a flat tire, and it is too much to get into without wine. Give me a minute to get these dinners warmed up and I'll tell you all about it while we eat prime rib."

He stepped to her and brought her into an embrace. "How about saying a proper hello to your man first?"

"Oh, I like proper—and not so proper, too." She leaned in and kissed his chin. "I needed this."

He lowered his mouth to hers and devoured her lips, lifting only when breathing became a necessity. "Hello." He smiled down at her. She was beautiful. All that wavy dark hair, curves that would make any pin-up model green with envy, and the absolute biggest heart on the planet.

"Hi. You know, just being in your arms makes the day better." She cocked her head. "When you called, you said you were having a bad morning. Did it get better?"

He rolled his eyes. "I think we should pour that wine."

"Oh, dear. That bad? Let me guess, it had something to do with Fenton." She took down the only two wine glasses he owned. They didn't match but did the trick.

He poured her half a glass and then did the same for himself. "Oh, yeah. He was in rare form. Came down to the office to threaten me and indirectly the team. That man wants me gone so badly I think he'd go through the damn good cops I have working for me to get to me."

Brianna leaned against the counter and arched an eyebrow, her wine glass stilled halfway to her mouth. He pointed to her. "Absolutely not. We've had this conversation."

"But why?" She put her glass on the counter. "He needs to know what this guy is doing."

"I've been up-channeling everything relevant to the Deputy Commissioner."

"Mavis or Lloyd?"

He laughed. "You mean Deputy Commissioner Duckworth or Deputy Commissioner Farrington?"

She snorted and picked up the takeout. "Yeah, sure. Potato-Potahto."

"Not all of us are on a first-name basis with the hierarchy of the Hope City Police Department." He watched her place the food onto separate plates.

"Don't think I didn't notice you didn't answer." She pointed at him with a fork and then turned to set the timer on his microwave.

"Fine. Mavis."

"Good, she's hell on wheels, according to Dad. Speaking of my dad..."

"Part of the conversation you had with your mother?" He chuckled when she dropped her head.

"I promised her when we have lunch next week that we could schedule a time for you to meet my family." She glanced up at the ceiling. "The force was not strong with me, Obi-Wan."

He laughed and took a drink of his wine. "This. This is why I'm falling for you."

"Aww, My *Star Wars* references are winning you over, aren't they? Admit it."

"No. Well, yes, I love the fact that you're as much as a movie nerd as I am, but it's the fact that you are a strong, independent woman who loves her mother enough to be the one with whom the force is not strong enough. Your heart is so big." He sat his glass down and folded her into him. "Speaking of big hearts, did you corner the councilman today?"

"I did. He said that the motion is once again not

on the agenda. I'm so mad that I'm about ready to sic Bekki on them."

"Your sister is the threat you'd wield?" He fought the smile that wanted to spread across his face.

She narrowed her eyes and tilted her chin. "Bekki is a good investigative reporter."

"I didn't say she wasn't, but you have much, much bigger guns in your arsenal."

"I do?"

"A commissioner, homicide detective times two, a JDET Sergeant, a DEA agent, and a captain on the Hope City Police Force, and all of that is *without* bringing your neighbors into the mix. Why would you choose Bekki?"

The timer on the microwave sounded, and she stepped from his embrace. "You want an honest answer?" She glanced at him and his mood sobered. Those beautiful blue eyes were serious as they stared at him.

"Always."

She removed one plate and put the other in the microwave before she set the timer and turned around to face him. "I don't mind using my dad to protect the people I love. Like telling him about Fenton. But when it comes to my business or even my life, having my family or my boyfriend's influence be the reason I succeed or not is a no-go."

Ryker barely heard her. In fact, he'd stopped listening after he realized she admitted to loving him. "You love me?"

"What?" Her eyes widened, and she stared at him, completely freaked out. He saw the moment she realized what she'd said. "Oh, well... you know what I mean." She turned away and grabbed silverware from the drawer.

He crossed the distance that divided them and placed his hands on her shoulders. "Don't hide from me, babe." He moved her hair and dropped a kiss on the pounding pulse in her neck. "I love you, too."

She twisted around in his arms. "You do?"

"How could you not know?" He dropped another feather-light kiss on her lips.

"Because you didn't tell me." She spoke between kisses.

"I just did."

"Yeah, you did." She wrapped her arms around his neck. "Are you hungry?"

"Starving." He slid his hands down to her ass and picked her up. She squealed and wrapped her long, luscious legs around him. It took seconds to carry her to the bedroom. He dropped them both onto the bed, but she scrambled to her knees and whipped off her shirt, flinging it across the room.

"Naked, now." She shimmied from her jeans while he was shucking his clothes. She shot her bra past his shoulder and wiggled out of her matching panties before she knee-walked to the side of the bed. "Is this for me?" She took his cock in her hand and stroked him from root to tip.

"Only you." He bent down and attacked her lips as his hands roved over her gloriously naked body.

She hopped off the bed and ducked his grab at her. "You, on your back, mister."

"What if I don't want that?" He stalked toward her.

"What do you want?" She licked her lips and stared at his shaft in his hand.

Easiest question in the world. "Mmm... everything."

She nodded as she answered, "Everything. I like that. Let's do that."

She climbed onto the mattress and crawled forward a bit. Looking back at him, she wiggled her ass. Mother of all things, the woman was irresistible. He reached for her and brought her hips toward him. She dropped to her shoulders. Her hand emerged between her legs and she guided him to her core. He hissed as he entered her. So tight. So fucking good.

Brie arched her back and moaned as he retreated and drove into her again. "Harder." Her demand was his pleasure. He grabbed her shoulders and pumped into her. Her hair swung with each thrust, sweeping the sheets in a dark fall.

He pulled out and moved her to her back, lifting her legs, holding them in a high V by her ankles. He found her center and rutted back inside her gripping heat. "God, you're beautiful." He dropped her legs and leaned forward. If he didn't kiss her now, he'd implode. She grabbed the back of his neck and beckoned him down to her. He pushed his knee forward and leaned on her leg, pressing it up to her shoulder, opening her wider as he drove home.

She broke the kiss and arched her neck. Panting, she dug her nails into his shoulders. "Yes!" She shattered around his cock. He didn't slow down; instead, he rode her through her orgasm, and when she finally opened her eyes, he moved away. He laid down on the bed and held his shaft.

She smiled wickedly and straddled his hips, sliding down onto him. He placed his hands on her hips and then slid them north. Her body was exactly what he loved in a woman. Wonderfully soft curves and full breasts. She lifted and lowered, moving her hips in a figure-eight at the bottom of her descent. The friction against his balls and cock damn near blinded him with need.

"I will not last if you keep that up."

"What? This?" She swiveled her hips at the base of his cock with just a bit more force.

"Brie..." He panted her name.

"Let yourself go. Fill me up. I want you inside me."

Ryker clutched her hips and slammed into her, thrusting from underneath as he pushed himself over the edge and shouted her name as he came.

He felt her fold above him and wrapped his arms around her. God, he'd never felt this way about a woman. He held her gently, casting his hands through her thick hair.

She started laughing and kissed his neck.

"What?"

"That wasn't everything. I can think of at least ten or twenty other positions we need to bring into our repertoire."

"Is that so?" He tickled her.

With a squeak, she fell to his side and cuddled

closer. "Yep, and then, when we have those down pat, we can always buy a copy of the Kama Sutra. I'm not sure I'm bendy enough, but hey, I can throw some more yoga workouts in."

He folded her into his arms and panted hard, trying to catch his breath. "Loving you will never be boring, will it?"

"Never." She laughed and snuggled into him. She was as out of breath as he was. They laid together in silence for several moments before she propped up onto her elbow. "Oh, Roger wants me to go in fifty-fifty with him and open another restaurant. All organic and sustainable foods. I think it may be doable, but I don't want to overextend."

He was still blissed the fuck out and the only thoughts he could manage were of doing all of what they'd just done again, and she was talking about a business deal. Damn, he had to be getting old. He narrowed his eyes as he stared at her. "And this popped into your mind now why?"

She scrunched her nose and furrowed her brow. "Let's see... I was thinking how good you made me feel, and how much I love you. It didn't really matter what kind of day I had as long as I ended up here with you. Then, of course, the day scrolled through my mind. My mother's call and agreeing to meet her next week for lunch and schedule a time for you to meet my family. Then I went a server down, we shuffled positions and I bussed to cover, I talked to the councilman with an apron on, which didn't bother me but seemed to irritate him. Then Roger talked to me about the idea he had. Hey, did you know he thinks my cousin is a billionaire?"

"What cousin? Jason? I think he's right."

"Jason's a billionaire?"

"Honey, he's the CEO of Guardian Security."

"And?"

"And it is global. It is bigger than the CIA and the FBI put together."

She rolled onto her back. "How come I didn't know this?"

"Probably because things like money don't matter to you."

She bobbed her head from side to side. "As long as I pay my bills and I have food on the table, I'm good. Beyond a point, money really isn't that important. But he wasn't talking about Jason, he was talking about Justin."

"I have no idea about that cousin. I take it you're not close?"

"No, not really. They grew up in Mississippi and there was a big argument between my grandmother and their father. From what my mom told me, the entire situation was ugly with a capital 'Ug'. Then my Uncle Chance was murdered. My Aunt Amanda raised eight kids by herself, although Dad and Mom made sure they called her once a month or so to make sure they were doing okay. We went down to Mississippi twice and they came up here once."

"Some families aren't close. It happens." His wasn't close. Not in the slightest.

"I don't think it was intentional, the distance. My mom and dad like Aunt Amanda. But sometimes life interferes." She sighed and groaned. "Then I found someone poked a hole in my tire."

"Say what?" He repositioned so he could see her better.

"It was dark, but I think either the inside rim of the tire gave up the ghost or someone put a hole in the tire with something sharp."

"I'll look at it tomorrow when I drop you off. If someone slashed it, you'll need to do a police report."

"It was probably some random thing. Seriously, it isn't a big deal. I needed new tires anyway."

"That is true, you do. Especially before winter sets in. Your old tires are almost bald, but if it was slashed, you'll do a report. Understand?"

She saluted him and huffed, "Yes sir, Captain Terrell, sir."

"You can be a smart ass, but I'm serious."

"I know and thank you, but I can handle this." She traced his brows with her fingertip.

He looked at her. "You really did have a day, didn't you?"

"Yeah, it was one thing after another. And did I mention I bussed tables, too?" She yawned, pulling her hand back to cover her mouth. "I need to go put dinner in the fridge unless you want to eat now."

"I'll take care of it. You go to sleep. I'll be right back."

She held him when he tried to get up. "No, you've got to be exhausted. You were the one who got called out last night."

"True, but I caught a power nap after I came home. I'm good. Besides, it won't take long." He dropped a kiss on her lips before he slid from bed and grabbed his jeans, shoving one leg in and then the other.

It took only moments to put the food away and

cork the wine. He cleaned the kitchen and turned off the lights, double-checking the locks on the doors and windows. Staring through the front window, he crossed his arms over his chest and bowed his head, thanking his maker for putting Brie in his life.

A strange thought torpedoed his consciousness. If Fenton hadn't relieved him of duty, he wouldn't have had the time to go to the gym and he would have never met her. The twisted trail of his life to this point hadn't prepared him for something as good and wholesome as Brianna King. A sudden dose of reality, *his* reality, broke across him like a wave pounding the beach. Good and wholesome were things that didn't last long in his life. Maybe, just this once, he'd be able to hold on to someone he loved.

CHAPTER 5

Ryker drove into the alley and parked behind her SUV. They both got out of Ryker's police sedan and walked to the right rear wheel of her truck.

"See." She leaned down and pointed to the slice in the tire. "But look here." She pointed to a bulge in the sidewall of her tire. "It could have erupted."

"No. Someone slashed your tire. The line is too clean. If it had exploded, it would have torn the rubber and made jagged edges. This isn't jagged." He ran his finger along the sharp edge.

"But why would someone want to do that?" She stood and put her hands on her hips.

"I couldn't tell you. I'm going to call Alston

Repair and Towing. He'll come get this old girl. Four new tires?"

She swung around and grabbed his arm. "And a spare, oh, and maybe a jack, too."

He narrowed his eyes at her. "You don't have a jack?"

"I did until about four months ago. I gave it to Tara. Some guy from the shelter needed one, and I wasn't using it."

He blinked at her. "Does that make sense when you say it out loud?"

She turned to look at him and burst out laughing. "Not in the slightest."

He released an exaggerated sigh, "Thank God. I was worried I'd fallen in love with a ditz." He dodged a quick flick of her hand toward his bicep.

"I'm not a ditz. I was planning on getting a new one."

He nodded and stared at the tire. "I'm sure you were."

She hip-checked him and then leaned into his side. She felt wonderful against him. "Do you need to go anywhere today?"

"Yeah, I have a couple things I need to do, but I'll call an Uber."

"Text me with the information."

She snorted. "I will not get Uber-snatched."

He tugged her in and kissed the top of her head, filling his senses with the scent of her citrus shampoo. "Everyone should have someone who knows where they are and where they're going. Safety isn't something I can compromise on. If you don't want to text me, text your sister or your mom. Just make sure someone knows, okay?"

"Okay." She tipped her head back, and he kissed her again, lingering in the solitude of the quiet alleyway.

"Consider getting a camera for above the back door. They are inexpensive and most of them store footage in the cloud for a year at a time."

"Isn't that overkill?" She glanced at the back door of the building.

He sighed. "Think about it this way. What if this had happened to Roger or one of the others who park here? What if whoever did that was still there when one of your employees went home? Having a camera back here pointed at the cars would provide additional security for them and for you."

Brie gave him a small nudge with her elbow. "Stop making sense, will you?"

"Not when it comes to your safety. Sorry."

She wrapped her arms around his neck. "I'll forgive you. Do you have time for a cup of coffee?"

He looked over her shoulder at his watch. "No, I have a meeting with a federal prosecutor this morning. I'll walk you to the door and wait until you get inside, but then I've got to go."

They meandered to the steps. He kissed her on the bottom step and again on the top. "I'll call you and let you know when Alston will come to pick the old girl up."

"Thank you." She pushed up on her toes and he bent down to kiss her again. "I love you." Her soft words sent a million joules of electricity through him.

Feeling like he could take on the entire city and win, he smiled down at her. "I love you, too. Be safe." He spun her and patted her on her perfectly pert ass.

She gave an indignant huff and slid the key into the top lock, then the middle, and finally, the third. She smiled and blew him a kiss as she walked in the door and shut it behind her. He heard the key lock being thrown and then the chirping as she deactivated the interior alarm system. He jogged down the stairs and headed to his sedan. Today was starting off one hell of a lot better than yesterday.

Maybe.

He stared at Mouse. The woman was twitching. She'd showered thirty minutes ago, not that you could tell. She was a wash of sweat and looked like death warmed over. "Detoxing hard. When do the feds show up?"

Terrence glanced at his watch. "Any time now. They pushed it back because a meeting they were in was running long." He leaned back against the table in the observation room. "Mouse can keep it together. She's fighting for her life right now. She knows it."

"We can try to get a doc here and give her a dose of Methadone."

Terrence shook his head. "If the feds come in and she can't form a coherent sentence, she won't get her deal."

"I talked to her about treatment. I've lined up a rehab facility in New York. Pulled in a fuckton of favors to get her into a bed tomorrow. She'll keep it together." He hoped.

Brody opened the interrogation room door. "Captain, Detective McBride is here. He has some information on Artog, Inc."

He nodded toward Mouse. "Monitor her?"

Terrence clapped him on the back. "Sure, I'll take my paperwork in there and do it. We'll get her through this. She's the key to Peña."

He followed Brody. "Your office?" Brody motioned to Detective McBride when he grunted and headed toward his desk.

The men came in and Brody shut the door behind him. "Have a seat." He waited until the detectives sat down before he leaned his forearms on his desk and pegged McBride with a stare. "We are working a possible conduit of cocaine into the city. According to my detectives, one entity that keeps bubbling to the top is a shipping company called Artog Shipping. When I briefed my major on it this morning, he indicated you might be able to provide some background. What can you tell me about the company?"

McBride groaned. "The gift that never stops giving. Congressman Dell is the majority shareholder of Artog Shipping."

He blinked as that tidbit of information registered. "As in the congressman who has been charged with interstate prescription drug theft and campaign fraud?"

Kyle McBride nodded. "The feds worked that portion of the case. I'm out of that end of it. But what we saw when we were working our investigation was that, occasionally, when a shipment with highly marketable prescription drugs went out to a major city, it would end up being stolen. The entire shipment, poof. Gone. Of course, it was usually a one-off, so it didn't ring on the city or county's radar. Artog Shipping has so many subsidiaries that, following the trail back to the primary company, owned by Congressman Dell, was difficult. Then the people getting rich got greedy and stole from their own backyard. We got lucky and found a trail of crumbs, crumbs the other cities wouldn't have been able to identify."

He leaned back and stared at the detective. "I wouldn't call it lucky. From what I heard it was damn good police work."

McBride looked uncomfortable with the compliment but muttered, "Thank you."

"So, we need to get with the FBI. If they are already looking into Artog, this will just be another feather in their cap." Brody rolled his shoulders as he spoke.

He hit his mouse and woke up his computer screen, glancing at the cases that were active and the detectives assigned. "I'll make the call to the feds, but until they pull us off this, make sure Cantrell and Lewis follow through with their informants and see what you can dig up from other sergeants working narcotics in the other precincts. If Artog is associated with prescription drugs and cocaine shipments, it may run deeper. I don't want us to sit on this if the feds are just going to drop it back in our lap, and if they take it, we might have a bit of information to make their lives easier." He glanced up at a tap at his door.

"Cap, sorry for the interruption, but Alston Towing called while you were in the interview room. Said they were leaving to pick up your SUV?" Amber cocked her head. "Thought you drove a sedan?"

"Not my vehicle, it belongs to a friend of mine. Thanks."

"No problem." She waved at Kyle and winked at Brody before she shut the door.

"Thank you, Detective McBride. I appreciate you stopping by."

Kyle stood, as did Brody. "No worries, sir. I was

in the area and decided Brody and Amber need to take me to lunch."

Brody chuffed and pointed at him. "My captain just gave me more work. You'll have to find someone else to buy your food, mooch."

Ryker cleared his throat. "Actually, those calls can wait for an hour or so."

Kyle laughed at Brody's crestfallen expression. "Captain Ryker, you just moved up to being my favorite officer on the entire force. Come on, tightwad, I want lunch at Horizon."

"Call ahead for a table, today is clam chowder day." He snapped his mouth shut, realizing what he'd just said. He glanced down at his desk blotter as if the scribbling there held the secrets to the universe.

"How do you know that?"

Brody's brow was scrunched together when Ryker glanced up. "It's the best damn chowder in town. What? Is it illegal to like chowder?"

"Ah, no, it's just that my sister owns that place and it's kinda out of the way from this part of town." Brody shrugged. "Strange that someone else would know about it."

"You're not the only one who owns a vehicle or

likes to eat, King. Get out of my office and shut the door on your way out."

"Yes, sir." Brody was out of the seat and at the door in a heartbeat.

"See, now you did it. You pissed off your boss," Kyle fake-whispered as he punched Brody in the shoulder on the way out the door. When it closed behind them, Ryker drew a deep breath. It was getting harder and harder to keep his and Brie's relationship under wraps. Perhaps it was a good thing that her mother was pressing for an intro-duction. Dealing with Brody and his brothers would be awkward, but they were all adults. Well, mostly. He watched as Kyle ducked from a head-lock Brody put on him and smiled as Amber shook her head and followed them out of the building.

He retrieved his cell and called Brie.

"Hey, good-looking," her voice purred across the line.

"Hey yourself. The tow truck is on its way to come get your vehicle. If they don't finish it today, I'll pick you up tonight. I don't want you to Uber."

"I'll take you up on that."

He chuckled. "What, no argument? Who are you and what have you done with the independent woman that I fell in love with?"

"She's still here. Things are just a little hectic again today. You gave the company my number so I can pay for the tow and new tires, right?"

"I haven't, but if you want me to, I will."

"Please do, I have the money to take care of it." She covered the phone with her hand and spoke to someone. "Sorry."

"I know you're busy. I just wanted to give you a heads up that Brody, Amber, and Kyle McBride are on their way. You'll have to dust off the owner's table."

"Are they? Wonderful! I haven't seen them in a couple weeks. I wish you could have come with them."

"Well, maybe after we do the introduction thing."

"You're not freaking out about that, are you?"

He chuckled softly. "Not at all. I love you and you come with a big family."

"So do you."

"But my family isn't close like yours."

"Well, if you meet my family, I need to meet yours."

"We can do that." He hated to think of it, and he'd put it off as long as he could, but he could arrange it. "I'll text you when the garage says the truck is ready."

"Thank you for taking care of that for me."

"Thank you for letting me help." He glanced up as Patel knocked on his door. He held up a finger. "I've got to go, babe. Love you."

"I love you, too. Bye."

"Enter."

Patel winced, "Cap, Fenton is in the parking lot and heading this way."

"Wonderful." He stood and rolled his shoulders. "Tell Lieutenant Theron to hold tight in the interview room with Mouse until the colonel leaves, please." The unexpected drop-ins by his supervisor's supervisor were getting old. But he'd grin and bear them until the team no longer reported to the asshole. Not that he had much of a choice.

CHAPTER 6

"Hey, Boss, call for you on line three," Lola yelled from the front of the restaurant and Brie barely heard it above the noise of the kitchen that was in full prep for a booked night.

It had been great to visit with Brody, Amber, and Kyle, but now she was right in the middle of prep. She didn't dare impede the chefs working in an orchestrated dance, but she was great at toting and fetching and keeping workstations cleared. She gave Lola a thumbs-up and moved a completed tray of desserts to the walk-in cooler before she trotted into her office and picked up the phone. "This is Brianna. May I help you?"

"You need to pay." The voice was low and deep.

Brie stood up straight and swiveled to look into

the kitchen, pushing her finger into her other ear so she could make out what the man said because there was no way she heard what she thought she heard. "I'm sorry, I didn't hear you. What did you say?"

"The tire was a wake-up call and a warning."

Her heart leapt into her throat, and she turned away from the door. "What are you talking about? A warning about what?"

"You need to pay. Wait for instructions." The line went dead.

"Boss?"

With a yelp, she jumped and clutched her hands to her chest, spinning. "Oh shit, Roger, you scared the crap out of me!"

"Whoa, maybe less caffeine tomorrow?" He arched an eyebrow and nodded to where she had the phone cradled to her chest. "I just got a call from the butcher. He's had issues with his walk-in cooler. We aren't getting our order for the next three days."

"What?" Her hand shook as she set the receiver back in the cradle and straightened her shirt.

"I called around and I can get us our order, but it is going to be more expensive." Roger dragged his hand through his hair. "Or I can call one of the big warehouse dealers."

"No, we support our local vendors. How much more?"

"Double."

"Double?" She sat down on her desk. "Okay, well, it's only three days. We'll manage."

"We can raise the menu prices," Roger offered.

"No, I can absorb three days. If it goes longer, we'll address what we need to do. In the meantime, do we have everything ready for tonight?"

"We do. The first reservations come in at five-thirty and then we have tables full until our last seating at nine."

She nodded and caught a glimpse of Lola as she power-walked through the kitchen. "Lola!"

The woman spun on her toes and headed for her office. "You bellowed?"

"Sorry, I did. The call you just patched through; I didn't get the name of the man who called. Did you?"

"No, I asked for a name, but they declined to give me one. Instead, they asked for the owner of the establishment."

"They didn't ask for me by name?"

"No. Why?" Both Lola and Roger looked at her like she'd lost her mind.

She tried to chuckle, but even to her own ears, the attempt fell flat. "I think they had the wrong number." God, she *hoped* they had the wrong number. But they mentioned the truck...

Lola shrugged, "Right, well, if they call back, I won't put them through unless they give me a name."

"Wait. No, put them through. I'll handle it. No need for you to get involved in this."

Lola cocked her head. "You sure? What did they say? You seem pretty rattled."

"I'm just jumpy today. Roger is blaming the caffeine, and he is probably right. Now, both of you go back to work, we have a restaurant to run." She made a waving motion with her hands and shooed them from her office.

She flopped into her chair and stared at the phone. A chill ran across her exposed skin. It was probably those two jerks that cornered her by her truck the other day. Well, they could go to hell. Two scraggly lowlife excuses would not intimidate her. But she would take Ryker's advice. Popping on the computer, she searched for outdoor security cameras, those with recordings that went to a cloud storage. It took thirty minutes to find the one she thought would work. One click later... boom, ordered and on its way.

She grabbed her cell and sent a text to Ryker.

> *New camera for outside ordered.*

His reply came back almost immediately.

> *You remembered?*

She rolled her eyes.

>*Ha ha.*

The bubbles floated for a moment before his reply came through.

> *Two years and you didn't buy a spare tire.*

She laughed and shook her head. She had no defense against that statement.

>*Some things just aren't that important.*

>*Obviously. Alston called. Your vehicle will be done today by five.*

>*I'll Uber and pick it up. I probably should stay at mine tonight.*

She also needed to water the plants, dust three weeks of non-use from the surface of everything, and battle whatever was growing in her refrigerator. She'd practically lived at Ryker's for the last month.

The phone in her hand vibrated and she jumped. Damn, that call had spooked her. She swiped the face and answered the call. "Texting wasn't doing it for you, sexy?"

"Nah, I'm more of a hands-on type guy." Ryker's voice was deep and smokey. It sent a sliver of excitement through her. "Babe, is there a reason you don't want to stay tonight?"

"Other than I'm paying rent on an apartment I haven't been to in a couple weeks?" She laughed and pushed her hand through her hair.

"Maybe we could think about you moving in with me permanently." Ryker's voice deepened. It did that when he was serious.

"I'd like that, but I still have, oh man, at least three months left on my lease. Besides, after you meet my family as 'the boyfriend', you might want to rescind that offer."

"What are you so worried about?"

"That they won't love you the way I do." She moved to her door and shut it, knocking out the kitchen noise.

"Well, babe, there is every possibility that Brody and Brock will never love me, and you know what? I'm okay with that." He laughed and then added, "I'm more concerned about the age difference. What will your parents think?"

"I can't see where it will be an issue. Really. You

know what, I've got an idea. Instead of waiting until next week, scheduling a date and then fretting until that day comes, why don't you just come with me to dinner on Sunday night?"

"Sunday as in three days from now?"

"Yeah. Let's just rip the bandage off and get it over with." She started pacing in the small space that held her desk and computer.

"If you're okay with it, I'm game. Will springing me on them cause a problem?"

"No. I can't see why it would."

"Then it's a date. Now, about tonight..."

"One night without me to warm your bed will not kill you."

"How do you know?" he groaned. "All right, but I may come to your house in the middle of the night just so I can sleep. I've grown fond of the way you wrap yourself around me."

"You're a furnace and I get so cold."

"I'll warm you up anytime."

She laughed. "That was corny."

"Did it work?"

"Yeah. Yeah, it did. I'll see you tomorrow night." She purred the promise into her phone.

"I love you, babe."

"And I love you. Be safe and catch all the bad

guys."

"I'll do my best. Bye."

She whispered a goodbye and disconnected the call. She was so happy, and yet a specter of fear raced just underneath that feeling. Was it too good to be true? God, she hoped not.

There was a knock on the door. "Brie, the dishwasher won't start."

She dropped her head back and stared at the ceiling. The joys of owning a restaurant.

Ryker dragged himself into his small house and flopped onto the couch, pushing back into his favorite corner of the sectional. He'd tossed his suit jacket over the far arm. Once he un-assed the couch, he'd hang it up. Maybe. He'd worked late last night since Brie didn't come over, and then he'd gone in early to take Mouse to rehab. By the time he made it back Fenton had been to the office twice and had the team going crazy. He'd taken personal time to drive his CI to New York so the bastard couldn't touch him for coming in at noon, but the ass still ranted like a madman.

After Fenton left, Patel and then Rayburn had

asked for a moment of time. They'd both recorded Fenton going off with their phones—insurance should the man do something like try to remove him again. Patel started the recording as soon as Fenton walked into the office and let it run until he left. It was good to know his people had his back, but damn it, he should have their backs, not the other way around.

His phone rang in his jacket. It wasn't Brie's ringtone. Shit. He sighed and reached for his suit jacket just as his front window shattered. A stab of pain sliced his arm. He dove and hit the floor and rolled, coming up on a knee with his service weapon in his hand. A dark blue or black late-model SUV hauled ass down the street. He jumped up and hurdled through the shattered window, pounding out to the street, aiming at the vehicle seconds before it careened around the corner.

"Oh, my God! Are you okay? You're bleeding!"

"Mrs. Thorn, get back inside! Call 911, tell them an officer needs assistance." She scurried back inside. Other neighbors backed up into their houses when he yelled for them to go back inside. *Come outside when you hear gunfire. Sheep, the world was made of fucking sheep cloaked in human forms.* He stood in the middle of the street and glared down at the spent shell casings. From where he stood, he could see inside the picture window. He could see the couch where he'd collapsed shortly after coming home. His jacket no longer hung on the arm of the chair. Fuck. He drew a shuddering breath. Someone had tried to kill him. *Who* and *why* were the questions he needed to answer.

The wail of a single siren and then more gained volume as the patrol cars raced toward his home. He saw the first car turn the corner and unclipped his badge from his belt, holding it up like a stop sign. The car screeched to a halt, and the doors opened. The officers took cover behind the doors. "Identify yourself."

"Captain Ryker Terrell, JDET Commander. I live there." He pointed to the small Craftsman. "Shooter has gone."

"Description?" One officer grabbed the radio.

"Late model SUV, possibly a Chevy. Blacked out rear and side windows. No description of the shooter. I didn't get a plate either."

The other officer walked closer. "Yeah, looks like you were busy getting shot at. You guys in JDET don't do things the easy way, do you?"

He gave the officer a quick up and down. "Do I know you?"

"No sir, but you know my sister. Detective Patel."

"Ah, she's an excellent officer." He turned to face the detective.

"She's a brat, just ask my mom." The guy nodded to his arm. "I think we need to get you to the ambulance."

"Ambulance?" He cast a glance around. Sure enough, an ambulance had appeared on scene and the techs were unloading the stretcher. Who was hurt? There were two other patrol vehicles now. He glanced down at his arm. How had he not felt all that blood dripping off his fingers?

He blinked, and the paramedics were by his side. "Sir, you need to lie down so we can look at your injury."

"I'm fine." He stared at the casings on the street and realized that maybe he wasn't fine. The brass wavered a bit, and his arm and shoulder burned like a bitch.

"Yeah, I don't think so, sir." The officer, Patel's brother, was suddenly in front of him.

The guy weaved. Oh fuck, it wasn't the officer who was moving, it was him. The world tipped radically to the right. "*Shit.*" He grabbed the patrolman.

CHAPTER 7

"**B**rie, you have a call on line two." Lola spun, her long black skirt swishing around her legs as she scurried back up to the front of the restaurant.

Brie wiped her hands from helping garnish plates and jogged into the office. There was no way one of her family would call during dinner rush. She drew a shaking breath before she answered, praying it wasn't the same disturbed caller from earlier.

"This is Brie."

"Brie, it's Amber. I just got done talking to Kallie and we agreed you need to know. Ryker is in the hospital."

Her ass landed on her chair. "What?"

"We promised you we'd never say a word, but I thought you should know. He was shot, and he's in surgery."

"Shot!" She screamed the word, and everyone in the kitchen stopped moving. She slammed the door shut. "Where are you?" She scrambled for her purse and jerked on her small desk drawer to open it.

"Brie, you can't come, or everyone is going to know. Brody is here, the entire team, our major. Fuck, even that asshole Colonel Fenton is here."

"God, what happened?"

"From what the neighbors said, a blue SUV stopped in front of his house and opened fire. From the blood spray in the front room, it looked like he was on the couch. He jumped through the shattered front window and tried to get a description of the vehicle. The responding patrols said he was bleeding but stable at the scene."

Blood spray! "Amber, *where* is he?"

"Sacred Heart. We're in the surgical waiting area. Fourth Floor, West Wing."

"I'm on my way."

She yanked open the door. "Roger, I have to leave."

"Is everything okay?" He was waiting outside her door.

"No. No, it isn't. My boyfriend is a cop. Someone shot him. Take care of the place? I don't know when I'll be back."

"We've got it, Boss. Call when you can."

She nodded and ran through the kitchen and out the back door. Fumbling in her purse for her keys, she didn't see the man standing beside her SUV.

"Well, look here. New tires. The pretty lady is just in time to watch."

Brie froze and elevated her eyes, her hand still in her purse. "You know, paying us for protection could keep this from happening." He withdrew a pocket knife and hoisted the blade. His friend rounded the hood and leaned next to the tire.

No, there was no fucking way. Not now. Not again. Her hand skimmed the handle of her nine-millimeter that she'd put into her purse yesterday when she'd gone to her apartment. Her father's and brothers' constant warnings about victims of opportunity sprang to her mind. No, she wasn't going to be harassed and victimized again. Her eyes narrowed, and she hissed, "Get away from my truck. You do not want to make me mad tonight."

"Why, what are you going to do about it?" The man raked her with his eyes. "You can pay us, and all this will stop. We'll protect you."

She removed the gun from her purse and pointed it at him. "You'll never get a penny from me. Now, leave and never come back."

The men's bug-eyed, slack-mouth response would have been comical at any other time. "Back up now, or I will shoot." She motioned with the weapon and the men raised their hands, slowly backing away. "Leave me and everyone who works here alone, or the next time we meet, you'll be holding your intestines." She used her free hand to feel around the bottom of her purse for her keys and finally depressed the fob, unlocking the driver's side door. Carefully, she got into the SUV, keeping the weapon pointed at the men. She put the car into gear and spun out of her parking slot. The weapon went back in her purse and she flew from the alley.

On any ordinary day, confronting those assholes and pulling a weapon would have been an almost insurmountable task. She wouldn't have had the guts to pull that gun. She would have given them her purse, the keys to her truck, anything to avoid the confrontation. But they were preventing her from getting to Ryker. She'd have pulled that trigger. God help her, she would have. Tears streamed down her face as she recklessly sped down the street. She wiped her cheeks and gunned it through a yellow light. The hospital wasn't far, but every second felt like hours.

The parking lot wasn't full, so finding a spot didn't take long. She grabbed her purse, shoved the gun into the glove box, and slammed the door, locking it with her fob on a dead run to the emergency room entrance. Skittering to a stop, she asked the first person who looked up at the admitting desk how to get to the surgical waiting room. *Elevator to four, take a left at the end of the hall and then make a right.* The words played on repeat as she waited for the elevator. *Four, left at the end of the hall, right.*

The car was blessedly empty and didn't stop until the fourth floor. She bolted down the hallway and turned right. About thirty people turned to look at her as she raced down the hall. She zeroed in on Brody. "Is he out of surgery? Is he okay?"

Brody's brow crunched. "Brie? What are you doing here? Who are you talking about?"

She thrust her hands out and spread them wide. "Ryker! Is he okay?"

The presence of a tall man beside her drew her attention. He had kind brown eyes and a wonderful smile. "Hi, I'm Lieutenant Theron. Ryker is still in surgery. The doctors said that the bullets caught him in the shoulder."

She grabbed onto the man's arm and held onto him like he was a life preserver. "Tell me what you know, please."

"This is an active investigation. We aren't releasing details." A bitter voice from behind her startled her, swinging her around. He was an older man in uniform. She glanced at the rank and knew this asshole had to be Fenton.

"Excuse me?" She glanced at the others in the room. None of the people gathered would meet her eyes. But they were staring, some with open contempt, at the man who addressed her.

"Oh... I get it. You're Fenton." She hefted her bag to her shoulder and stared at him with the disgust that had been brewing for months. "What are you going to do, Colonel? Are you going to blame Ryker for getting shot in his own house? Are you going to spin it that he was incompetent for sitting on his couch? Or you could relieve him of command for being off duty at home and then try to paint him and his team as ineffectual as they bust their asses to make this city safer. Let's compare arrest records, shall we? Why don't you whip out your limp dick, Colonel Fenton, and let everyone see how lacking you truly are? If anyone here is inept and unsuitable for duty, it's you. Now, if you'll excuse me, I'm not talking to you, I was talking to––"

The man's face flushed red and a vein on his forehead bulged. "Who the hell do you think you are?"

"My name is Brianna King." She flung her arm toward the surgical doors. "I'm in love with Ryker Terrell, and just so we are clear, you, sir, are a complete ass."

"King." Fenton sneered.

"Yes, she's my daughter." Brianna pivoted at her father's voice. Brody and Amber stood to his left, Deputy Commissioner Duckworth to his right. "Brie, I think you need to take a walk with Amber and cool down." Her father's voice left no room for argument. She looked back at the doors that were still closed. "I'll send someone for you if anything happens."

Amber nodded toward the hall. When they turned the corner, Amber spun and hugged her.

"Oh, my God, Brie, you told Fenton to whip out his dick!"

She chuffed a small laugh. "He's such an asshole to Ryker. I just... God, Amber, my father's going to kill me. Hell, Brody and Ryker are going to kill me, too."

"Well, you can only get killed once, right? But the look on Brody's face when you went after Fenton, that was nothing but pride."

"Yeah?" They strolled down the hall, finding a small room with vending machines.

"Oh, yeah. It will take him a couple minutes to digest all of that before he realizes you said you were in love with his captain."

"God, I said that, didn't I?"

"Oh, yeah. *Loudly*." Amber shoved a bill into the machine and punched a button for a soda. She popped the top and handed the can to her. "Drink. You need the sugar. It helps when you're freaking out."

Brie took a sip and shook her head. "Why would anyone shoot at him?"

"Well, he's the commander of the JDET team. There are many people who have grudges against us. But you don't need to worry about that. We will find out who did this and why. I know you probably haven't thought about this, but is there someone that you should call for him? A family member?"

She stared at the top of the soda can. "He's not close to his family, but I know their phone numbers are on his cell. I saw them when I was scrolling through it one night."

"Wow, it really must be love if he lets you scroll through his phone."

Amber chuckled, and Brie's face heated. They were lying in bed after a fabulous round of sex and he was showing her pictures on his phone. He'd gone to the kitchen to get them some water, and she'd snooped. "Do you have his cell? I can call them."

"I don't, but we can find out where it is. In the meantime, I have orders to parade you around the hospital until called." Amber linked their arms together and tugged her gently, moving them into the hall.

"Dad is so going to murder me."

"Yeah, probably. And is it wrong to be happy that the family focus is finally off me?" Amber giggled when Brie groaned.

Ryker blinked his eyes and jolted, trying to orient himself. A soft hand landed on his arm and he jerked. A nurse?

"You're in recovery. You just came out of surgery. The doc will be here to talk to you soon. How's your pain level?"

He shook his head. "Fuzzy."

"That's expected. You're lucky Doc Phillips was on call. He's the best orthopedic surgeon in the city. Is there someone in the waiting room you'd like me to get for you?"

"Brianna." He croaked the word, swallowed, and then said her name again.

"I'll go get her. You rest." The nurse patted his forearm again and dipped out of the curtain-partitioned area.

A rotund man as round as he was tall waddled into the room after she left. "Captain Terrell, I'm Dr. Phillips. How are you feeling?" He came and stood beside the bed and tented the material of the sling they'd placed Ryker's arm in, taking a peek and nodding. He didn't wait for Ryker to speak but continued on. "The bullet shattered your shoulder socket. It definitely made a fine mess, but we performed a total shoulder arthroplasty."

"A what?" He narrowed his eyes at his doctor and then craned his neck to see his shoulder.

"Basically, we removed the damaged portions of your shoulder joint and replaced the damaged sections with artificial implants."

He wiggled the fingers of his injured arm before he asked, "Will I be able to stay on the force?"

"I don't see a reason why you couldn't. As a captain, you're primarily behind a desk, right?"

He nodded. For the most part, he was or could be. Fucking hell.

"How did this happen?" The doc opened a computer and focused on the screen.

"Drive-by shooting."

The doctor stopped and turned to him. "You work the gang task force?"

"No sir." He worked JDET, and why the fuck would someone do a drive-by of his house? Fuck, what if Brianna had been there? He screwed his eyes shut tightly. He needed to talk with Theron and King. There had to be something, some reason this happened. One he couldn't produce through the drug-induced haze.

"You'll be in the hospital for a day or two. Tomorrow, we'll take you to radiology and make sure that joint is being good and staying in position. We'll immobilize your shoulder for the first portion of rehab. That's to make sure your muscles and tendons have a chance to heal. You can take off the sling to shower or at the instruction of your PT and for no other reason. Otherwise, you'll mess up my work, and I hate going back into someone I've already fixed. Screw this up and I'll make one arm a couple inches shorter than the other."

He glanced at the doctor. The man's neck wiggled when he talked, but damn if he didn't believe the guy. Tough little bastard.

"How long does it take to heal?"

"I won't blow smoke up your hospital johnnie, this injury is going to take time to mend. Six weeks in the sling, and you and your physical therapist are going to be on a first-name basis, but you're strong and healthy, you'll bounce back quickly. Desk duty starting in three weeks, reevaluation after four months. If everything goes well, we can release you to full duty in six months. Some patients can take up to a year to recover fully."

"I don't have that long." He needed to be back with his people and out in the field.

"Then I suggest you follow your PT's exercise and rehab schedule to the T." The doctor shut the

lid on the computer. "I've ordered anti-inflammatory medications and a cold therapy machine
which circulates ice water around your joint in a
tubing under a pad. It will help with discomfort
and swelling."

He lost interest in what the doctor was saying
the moment he saw her. Tears shimmered in her
beautiful blue eyes as she moved forward. He
raised his good hand, careful of the IV that skew-
ered the back of his hand.

"Oh, God." She took his hand gently and
dropped her forehead to his.

The doctor chuckled and cleared his throat.
"And that's my cue to leave. I'll see you tomorrow
afternoon after I read the x-rays."

Ryker didn't acknowledge the doctor; his entire
focus stayed on Brianna. "I'm okay." He repeated
the words over and over as she cried. Her *'I love
you*'s and his meshed into soft kisses.

Finally, she moved away and wiped her tears.
"I'm sorry. I promised myself I wouldn't cry."

"You can cry, I'm sure it upset you. Who called
you?" God, he wanted to hold her next to him.

"Amber. It was a joint decision between her and
Kallie."

"It was the right decision."

She half-laughed, half-sobbed. "I was so frightened, and then when Fenton..."

"What?" He watched her face flame. "Brie, what did you do?"

"I might have told him off."

"Good for you." He closed his eyes for a moment before a thought struck him. "So, Brody knows now?"

"Ah, yeah. Brody, your entire team, my dad, the Deputy Commissioner, and a couple people I'm pretty sure were here for someone else."

"You made a fuss, huh?"

"Son, she told Colonel Fenton to whip out his dick and show the entire team what he was lacking." Commissioner King's voice preceded him into the room. Out of habit, Ryker struggled to sit up, sending a blast of pain through his shoulder and arm.

He hissed, and Brie hovered, trying to help. "Do you need something for the pain?" Brie's hand trailed down his cheek.

He shook his head and fell headlong into her eyes. "No. I'll be fine."

"Brie, maybe you could go tell the rest of the team that he's okay. I'd like a word alone with Captain Ryker." He watched as father and daughter stared at each other. Finally, she nodded. "I'll be right back." She leaned down and kissed him then ducked between the curtains.

Commissioner King put both hands in his slacks pockets and rocked back on his heels. "What did the doctor say?"

"He replaced my shoulder, long rehab, but I'll be ready for desk duty in three weeks."

Brie's father nodded. "Exactly how long have you been having problems with Fenton?"

"Sir?"

"Answer the question. You look coherent enough to understand what I'm saying."

"Since I took the position." Which was the truth. Fenton had a hard-on for him as soon as he started forming the team.

Commissioner King nodded and stared at the IV stand as he spoke. "Here's what we're going to do. From now on, you report directly to Mavis. JDET is now under Central. The politics and economics of the situation be damned. Fenton and Hughes are no longer in your chain of command. As there seems to be a conflict of interest brewing, Deputy Commissioner Duckworth will be your immediate supervisor, Deputy Commissioner

Farrington will be your next level. That removes me from direct supervision."

"Sir, Major Hughes did everything he could——"

An elevated hand stopped his words, midstream. "Hughes is a good man. Thank you for the confirmation." Chauncey slid his gaze and pegged him with a level stare. "How long have you and my daughter been involved?"

"Three months. We met when I was removed from JDET."

"And when were the two of you going to announce this relationship?"

"Sunday at dinner." He swallowed hard. "I love her, sir. With everything I am."

Brie's father nodded again. That nod could mean anything from *I hear you* to *Fuck off and die.*

"Save me the effort of looking it up in your personnel files. How old are you?"

"I'll be forty-seven this year." He drew a deep breath and waited, knowing what was coming next.

"Then you are damn well old enough to understand my next comment, and this comes from her father, not your commissioner. You hurt my daughter and this drive-by will pale compared to what I'll do to you."

He blinked. *Not. What. He. Expected.* "I'd never intentionally hurt her. You have my word."

Chauncey stared at him for a moment. "Dinner is at six on Sunday. I'd advise you not to be late." The Commissioner turned but glanced back at him. "Get yourself healed up. Your position on JDET is secure. Lieutenant Theron will man the ship until you get back."

"Yes, sir." He closed his eyes as the curtains filled in the big hole left by the one hell of a big man. Damn it, it had been a long, long day.

CHAPTER 8

Brianna gripped Ryker's phone and lifted it. "Thank you for this." It was the first time she'd talked to Brody since her rant against Fenton. Most of the team was still in the waiting room, all wanting to pay their respects to their captain. Brody nodded down the hall and they strolled until they were out of earshot. Brody stopped and leaned against the wall.

"So, you and the Captain, huh?" He shoved his hands into his pockets and did everything he could to avoid looking at her.

"Yeah."

He scraped the toe of his boot against the tile floor. "How long has this... thing been going on?"

"Thing?"

"You know what I mean." He crossed his arms and leveled a pissed off stare at her.

"Wait, why do you care?"

"He's my boss, Brie! You could've cuddled up with a half-million other men in this city, but you put the moves on my boss! Do you realize what kind of position that puts me in? What type of mess this puts Dad in?"

She lifted a hand. "Whoa, right there. First and foremost, I had no idea he was your boss. We met when he'd been removed from command of your team. I didn't ask what he did, and he never asked if I was the commissioner's daughter. I love that man, so I'm sorry my relationship with Ryker puts you in an awkward position, but I'll be damned if I'm going to walk away from the best thing that has ever happened to me to please my little brother." She hissed the words at him. Even trying to be quiet, a few heads from the waiting area turned their direction.

Brody tightened his fists and started pacing. "Do you realize how old that man is?"

"I know exactly how old he is. Why?"

"Brie, think about it. If you had children today, he'd be like seventy by the time they were twenty!"

She jerked up and snapped her mouth shut.

The words she wanted to say slammed against her brain, demanding to be let loose. "What did you just say?"

Brody didn't catch the warning in her voice. He just continued pacing. "He's in his late forties now, you'll be a widow by the time you're fifty, with kids and bills. Hell, you got to look at this rationally."

Her palm found his face and connected with a resounding smack. All conversation on the floor stopped. He lifted his hand to his cheek and narrowed his eyes at her. She pointed a finger at him. "You have no right. *None.* I don't know where this relationship is going, but I know one thing— whatever happens between us is our business, *not yours.* Never yours. You judgmental asshole! You don't want me to bring up your relationship with Amber, do you? No, I didn't think so. You don't get to dictate my life. Hell, you don't get any input into my life! So take your sanctimonious bullshit and stick it up your ass, Brody." She spun on the ball of her foot and headed back to the surgical ward.

"Brie." He jogged after her and spun her around. "I just don't want you to get hurt."

"The only thing hurting me is your attitude. You know him. You know the man he is!" She shook off his hand. "Just leave me alone. I can't do this with you right now."

"Brianna." She spun at her mother's voice. Brie launched herself into her mom's arms. All the worry, the terror of the call, the stupid low-life scum threatening her, and her scuffles with Fenton and Brody exploded into a barrage of tears. She felt herself being led to a bench where her mother held her and stroked her hair as she cried. Her mom thrust a tuft of tissue into her hand. She blew her nose and hiccupped, "I'm sorry." Her mom shushed her and continued to stroke her hair. "Brody pissed me off."

"Yes, I heard. Normally, I'd suggest that you need to apologize, but in this case, I think my son needs to pull his head out of his ass."

"Mom!" She sat up and gaped at her mother.

"What? It's the truth. I heard most of what he said about Ryker. I agree with you. One hundred percent. Your relationship has nothing to do with Brody or your father or the force." She tugged more tissue from her purse. Her mother pointed to her own eyes and whispered, "You need to de-raccoon yourself."

Brie chuffed a laugh and dabbed at her eyes. "Better?"

"Much. Now, tell me how your man is doing."

"They did a shoulder replacement. He looks good. Pale and tired, but good. The nurse said she'd come get me when they transferred him to the post-op ward."

"He was shot?"

"Yeah. At his house."

"Well, neither of you will stay there for the foreseeable future. I can get the guest room ready and you can have your old room. They wouldn't dare come to our house." Hannah dropped her hands into her lap and smiled as if she had the entire situation handled.

"Ah, Mom, I don't want you to take any offense at this, but... no."

Her mother blinked and then broke into a wide smile. "Spoken like a woman in love. We will need to find a place for him to stay and recuperate."

"I agree."

"Is his family here? Maybe they have a suggestion." Her mom twisted to look down the corridor at the people milling around. Amber was talking to Brody. No, make that scolding Brody. She couldn't hear, but she could see Amber's attitude from where they sat.

"Brie?"

"Oh, sorry." What were they talking about? Ryker's family. "No, I don't think so." She toyed with the phone. "I wasn't sure if I should call them without his permission."

"Why?"

"They aren't as close as we are. A gut feeling based on things not said. There may be substantial discord running through the family." She looked at the screensaver on his phone. It was a selfie of them together at the inner harbor boardwalk.

"Is that him?" Her mother pointed to the picture.

"Yes. This is Ryker. Mom, he is so good to me and I love him so much. What Brody said was hurtful."

"How much older is he?"

"Thirteen and a half years." She traced her finger over the picture.

"Oh goodness, that isn't bad. I have a friend who married a man twenty-five years older than she was. He was fifty when they married. First serious relationship for her and second for him. They had four kids and at seventy-five he is still as handsome and strong as he ever was. A silver-haired fox. They have had twenty-five years together and are still going strong." Her mother pushed her hair behind her ear and smiled at her. "If you love that man, you grab ahold of him and you don't let anyone or anything stand in the way of what you have together."

"Brody said it would cause problems for Dad."

"Brody needs to mind his own business. If your father has issues with your relationship with Ryker, he'll tell you and Ryker, not Brody." Her mom snorted. "Believe me, two people in love is a minor bump on the mountain of bullshit he has to deal with on a day-to-day basis."

"Mom!" Shocked, she glanced around the hall. "That is the second time you've cussed in less than thirty minutes."

Hannah chuckled. "What? You think I don't know how to use curse words? I do, and I let them fly when I need to make a point or get someone to listen to what I'm saying, and that's what you need to do. *Listen*. Your relationship with this man won't cause any hardship for your father. If it does, he'll take steps to mitigate it. As far as Brody's problems, that's on Brody. Your brothers are protective. You ripped him a new one, and from the looks of it, Amber is confirming your tirade." Hannah nodded down the hall. Amber's hands were on her hips and she was talking a mile a minute. "Just give him a while to lick his wounds. He'll figure out he was way off the mark and apologize. And if he doesn't, I'll show him the light of day."

"I was going to bring Ryker to the house on Sunday and introduce him to you and Dad and whoever else came to dinner." She dabbed her eyes again. "Did I get it all?"

Her mother took a fresh tissue and dabbed under her eyes. "There are no more mascara rings."

Brie laughed and stared down at the phone in her hand. "Should I call his family?"

Her mother shook her head. "Well, I would want to know if my child was hurt. Would you want to know if one of the boys was shot?"

"Yes, I would." She opened the phone and scrolled down his list of contacts to the one that read *Father*. She punched the number in and put the phone to her ear.

"Hello?"

"Mr. Terrell?"

"No, my name is Benjamin Ganas. I take it you're calling about Ryker?"

"Ah, yes sir, my name is Brianna King, I'm Ryker's... girlfriend. I'm calling to let you know that Ryker was injured in the line of duty. He's going to be okay, but he's had surgery. He's at

Sacred Heart and is being moved into the post-surgical ward."

"Did he ask you to call me?" The man's question was more like a demand.

"No sir. My mother and I felt we would want to know if a member of our family was injured, so I called you."

There was a pause before he spoke again. "Brianna was it?"

"Yes sir."

"Thank you for the call."

She lowered the phone and frowned. The man had hung up. "Wow, okay, that was weird."

"How so?" Her mom looked at her expectantly.

"Well, he was rather distant." Uptight and cold were the words she'd use.

"Some people don't show emotion easily." Her mom patted her arm.

She nodded. *Yeah, maybe.* She bit her lip and glanced down the hall. Damn, she hoped making that call wasn't a mistake. Ryker had so much on his plate as it was, he didn't need family drama thrown into the mix.

∽

Ryker winced as he pushed the button to lift his bed up straighter. He'd asked the nurse to send in Terrence and Brody. He needed to talk to them without Brie present.

There was a knock and Terrence opened the door, stepping inside with Brody on his heels. "Well, shit, you don't look too bad." Terrence walked up and shook his left hand carefully. Brody just nodded from the foot of the bed.

So be it. He directed his question to his lieutenant. "What have we learned from responding patrols and the crime scene techs? Who has the case?"

"Shootings Division has the case. Detectives Callaway and Forsythe. They are waiting to talk to you." Terrence nodded toward the door.

"Call them in." Brody moved to leave. "No, Terrence, you go get them. I need a moment with Sergeant King."

Terry whistled and then chuckled. "Going to get it again, aren't you, Sergeant King?"

Brody flipped off Terrence, causing the man to let loose with a rumble of laughter. "You're not my type, King." He opened the door and walked out.

Ryker pinned his sergeant with a stare. "Are we going to have a problem?"

Brody's gaze met his. He couldn't read what was going on behind those blue eyes that looked so much like Brianna's, but what he could do was confront his sergeant about the situation.

"No sir." The response was terse and clipped.

"What did he mean by get it again?"

"Family issues."

Right. That was a door closing in his face. Not like he'd let that deter him. "Yeah, well, here's a bit of news for you: I love your sister. I'm not going anywhere, so that makes me family adjacent. You report to Terrence and then to the Deputy Commissioner, and before her, it was to Major Hughes. I didn't change your supervision back to me after my return to duty because at first, I was swamped trying to clean up the mess Fenton had dropped in my lap. *Then*, when I figured out who Brie was, it was self-preservation. I'd never put *my* command or *your* position in jeopardy because of this relationship. So, suck up whatever objections you have about me and your sister and climb on board, or get the hell out of my way. I don't give a shit which way you fall. Brianna is it for me and you doing the silent angst thing is done. Copy?"

Brody stared at him for several long moments. "Loud and clear."

The door opened and Terry peeked in. His lieutenant spoke over his shoulder to someone, "No blood, you can come in."

He stared at his friend and narrowed his gaze. Terry would make a joke out of anything. It was his way of reducing the tension in the room. Only it didn't work this time, it just made things more awkward. Two men stepped in behind Terrence.

"Captain Terrell, I'm Detective Callaway, this is Detective Forsythe." They flashed their badges and Ryker acknowledged them. "We need to find out exactly what happened at your house this evening."

Ryker shifted in his bed and winced. "I came home as usual."

"Did you notice anyone following you, anything out of normal on the drive home?"

"No. I'm very cautious. There was no one tagging me. I parked in the driveway and waved to Mrs. Thorn, my neighbor. She was doing whatever it is she does with her plants. I unlocked my kitchen door, walked inside, flipped the deadbolt, and dragged my ass into the living room. I took off my jacket, flopped it over the arm of my couch like I do every night, and dropped into the corner of the couch to veg for a couple minutes."

Forsythe looked up from his notebook. "The corner of the sectional nearest the kitchen?"

Ryker shook his head. "No, the one closer to the hall. It's where I always sit."

Both Callaway and Forsythe scribbled something down. "Then what happened?"

Ryker thought carefully. "I got a phone call, so I slid across the couch to grab it from my jacket. That's when all hell busted loose."

"Do you have any idea who called you?"

"No, but it would be on my caller ID. If I hadn't reached for the phone, the bullets wouldn't have come anywhere near me." Ryker stopped and swiveled his head from the two detectives toward Terrence. "Where is my phone?"

"Brie has it," Brody answered. "I'll go get it." He darted from the room.

"Do you think someone called you to get you into a position to take you out?" Terrence spoke the question that was on his mind but then continued, "Your number is unlisted."

Callaway looked up from his notepad. "Have you given it out to anyone recently?"

He shook his head but then stopped. "No, but Mouse did."

"Who's Mouse?"

"Mouse is my CI that is now a linchpin witness in a major case. She gave my number to a prostitute working the streets. Alice is her name. She texted me Mouse's pickup location, and I sent a team to go get her."

"Do we know Alice's actual name? Where to find her?" Callaway scribbled as he asked.

Ryker shook his head. "No. I'd start at the Cottages and then the warehouses where the homeless congregate. That was where Mouse said she'd been hiding."

The door opened and Brody walked to the head of the bed, giving Ryker the phone. With his good hand, he swiped the screen and entered his code. He hit the call log and winced at the top outgoing call. His stepfather? Damn it.

Forsythe must have noticed the reaction. "Do you recognize the number?"

"No, sorry, my shoulder twinged a bit. Here is the cell number from which I received the text to pick up Mouse. This is the unanswered call that I was moving to answer when they took shots at me." He handed them the phone so they could write down the number attached to the pickup text and the last one on his call log. "Should I try to call it back?"

Forsythe shook his head. "No, we don't want the players to know we've connected the dots. Besides, this is probably a burner phone. We'll have tech run it and figure it out. If we go that route, we'll let you know. Until then, pretend it doesn't exist."

He nodded and dropped the phone onto his lap. "Maybe you can ping it, see if it is still active."

"We threw up a geofence around your neighborhood when the shooting happened which trapped all the numbers pinging in that area. If this number was in your area, getting a warrant won't be a problem, but let us worry about that. You're not the investigator on this, you're the victim," Callaway reminded him. *As if he needed it.*

Forsythe continued with the questioning. "Anything about the shooter's vehicle that you can remember?"

"It was a dark blue SUV. Blacked-out windows with chrome bumpers, early nineties model, but shiny and well-maintained. I didn't get a plate. I made sure the casings in the middle of the street were undisturbed until responding patrols arrived."

Callaway nodded. "Yeah, we saw where you

were standing. What's the prognosis on your injuries?"

"The doc rebuilt my shoulder. I'll be back at work in three weeks. Desk duty."

"Well, I for one am damn glad we're doing the investigation instead of homicide. No offense to your brother, man." Callaway winked at Brody.

Brody looked straight at him and nodded. "Yeah, I'm damn glad it's you, too." Brody turned his attention to the detectives and added. "What do you need from us?"

"Nothing. Once we get a trace on this number, we may need some coverage on surveillance."

"Whatever you need, you've got it," Terrence assured him.

The detectives left, and the door closed behind them. Ryker leaned to the side, trying to ease the pain in his shoulder. "Have we checked on Clare Edelman? What about her husband?"

Brody answered, "I checked on Clare this afternoon. She's out of general pop. It was the best we could do without more probable cause. The marshal in charge of her husband's case has assured me he's safe and aware of the situation. But I have to ask, why in the hell would Peña go after you?"

"I don't know. Maybe he thought Mouse was with me? God only knows what Alice said if they got to her."

"Yeah, but calling your cell to put you in the line of fire... Cap, that is almost like whoever was shooting at you knew what your routine was." Brody rubbed his stubble. "Cap, do any of your neighbors have security cameras?"

Ryker blinked. "You think they've been watching me."

Brody nodded his head. "I do."

"Mrs. Thorn has a system. She lives across the street. Some kids were messing with her flowers and she had her son put it up. I don't visit much with the other neighbors, so I'm not sure."

Terrence dropped a hand on Brody's shoulder. "Let's go talk with Mrs. Thorn and canvas the neighborhood."

"Sounds like a plan, but in the morning. It is way too late to be knocking on Joe Citizen's door, especially after a shooting in the hood. It would be our luck we'd get taken out by a John Wayne wannabe and then Ryker would have to run his own investigation." Brody smiled at him. It would seem the surprise relationship had finally settled around his sergeant.

"Morning would be better. I haven't lost a cop on my watch and I don't want to start with either of you. We should give Forsythe and Callaway a heads-up," he reminded his team they were not the lead on this matter.

"And we will, Cap, as soon as we know whether we have any information to give them. No sense sending them on the trail of a red herring." Brody smiled at him.

"Fine, getcha assess out of here and send in Brie, would you?" He spoke directly to Brody.

"I damn near had to tie her to the chair to keep her out when I retrieved your phone." Brody rubbed the back of his neck. "We good?"

"We're good." Ryker nodded and winced. The pain medication was definitely taking its time to kick in.

Terrence winked at him from behind Brody. "Rest and get yourself healed up."

CHAPTER 9

Brie hugged her mom goodbye and sat patiently in the small waiting area in the post-surgical ward. Ryker's team had drifted away but only after their lieutenant, the kind man who'd explained things to her when she first arrived, had announced their boss would be fine and no one else would be able to see him tonight.

The sound of footsteps turned her attention to the hallway. Four tall men walked in unison to the nurse's desk. One was attired in a three-piece suit, one wore jeans, a maroon tee-shirt, and work boots, another wore workout clothes, and the fourth looked as if they had dragged him from bed. They had similar features—sandy brown hair, high cheekbones, broad shoulders, and long legs. Their features were so alike, relatives... brothers probably. All four leaned forward when the one in the three-piece suit talked to the nurse. *Ah, they probably just found out about a loved one's surgery.*

She closed her eyes and relived the phone call she'd received from Amber. The confusion and then the terror that raced through her and then the profound urgency to be with Ryker were still so fresh and raw. She knew what that family was going through and she wouldn't wish it on anyone.

"Excuse me. Are you Brianna?"

Her eyes popped open. The men from the nurse's station formed a semi-circle around her chair. Not close enough to make her feel uncomfortable, but she stood up anyway. "Yes."

A soft smile spread across his face. "I'm Xander, this is Killian, Elias, and the one on the end is Dimitri."

Brie glanced at the other men and then looked back at... *Xander.* "I'm sorry, should I know you?"

The smile fell from the man's lips. "Ah, perhaps not, although we'd hoped. We are Ryker's half-brothers."

Brie smiled and ran her hand through her hair.

"Oh, I'm so sorry. I knew he had a large family, but we haven't talked much about you."

"There are the four of us besides Ryker. How is he?"

"He's out of surgery and awake. They just moved him up here and his lieutenant and sergeant are with him now." She motioned to the room as the lieutenant walked out. He smiled at her and headed down the hall in the opposite direction.

"Our father said that you were his girlfriend?"

"I am." They were more than that, but she didn't share that information. She motioned to the chairs. "Would you like to sit down?"

"Thank you." They all took a seat and then Xander spoke again. "What happened?"

"Well, I just have the broad picture. From what I understand, he was at home and someone shot at him through the front picture window."

The lieutenant and two other men went back into Ryker's room. She sighed and realized Ryker's brothers had been watching the door, too.

Finally, the one in work clothes, Killian, cleared his throat. "I knew being a cop was dangerous, but damn it, I never thought he'd be shot. I mean, he's a captain. Isn't that a desk job?"

She chuckled. "For some it would be, but he's the Captain of the Joint Drug Enforcement Team. He is in the field with his people. Most of their busts are enormous and usually very successful. He and his team have received at least five meritorious service awards." Probably more, but that was the count she had since Brody started working on the team. Her dad was damn proud of the work the team had done and bragged on them often.

All four men exchanged looks with each other. "What?" She had a feeling she'd let a cat out of the bag.

She bit her bottom lip and glanced at the door just as Brody walked out. She jumped up. "Is everything okay?"

He held up a hand, stopping her from asking another question. "Everything is fine, Brie. Do you have Ryker's phone?" Brody examined the men who stood when she did. He stuck his hand out to the nearest man. "Detective Brody King."

Xander performed the introductions again. "Are you related to Brianna? You have a striking resemblance."

Brody smiled politely and glanced at her before he answered, "I'm her brother."

Brie could see the confusion and unasked questions in Brody's expression. "They are Ryker's brothers."

Brody blinked. That Ryker had brothers startled Brody. She could read him well enough to know the info had set him back a step. "Brothers? Cool. Good to meet you." He turned his attention to her. "We'll be done shortly, but I know the nurses will probably kick you to the curb soon as it is well after visiting hours. Why don't you go home and come back in the morning? You look exhausted."

She shook her head adamantly. "It is going to take a crowbar and one hell of a lot more muscle than a fussy nurse to get me out of here before I see him again."

Heat rose to her face when a spattering of laughter from the men beside her registered. Brody chuckled, too. "Okay, okay. I'll take the phone, and if the nurses try to call security, let me know and I'll flash my badge for you."

"Thank you." She handed him Ryker's phone and ran a shaking hand through her hair.

"I guess we won't be able to see him tonight. Would you mind taking my card? If you could give us updates, we'd appreciate it."

She glanced at the engraved card and pocketed

it. "I'd be glad to do that. I'm sure Ryker will call you tomorrow."

Xander smiled, although it didn't go all the way to his eyes. "I would like to believe so, however, our past has been rocky. We're trying to close the gap between us. It's been difficult."

Brie saw the honesty in Xander's face and reflected in his brothers' expressions. "I'll do whatever I can to help you." Not being close to family was almost impossible for her to fathom. Her life teemed with all the messes and joys of brothers, sisters, and neighbors being in everyone's business. Sure, there were differences and squabbles, but she'd do anything for her family, and if she had a problem, all she had to do was pick up a phone. It appeared these four brothers had that. Why didn't Ryker?

They said goodnight and walked in pairs down the almost vacant hallway.

"Brie? You okay?" Brody walked up to her.

"What? Oh, yeah, I'm fine." She rubbed her arms. "When can I see him?"

"Now. I'll run interference with the nurse and buy you some time, but you will get kicked out sooner rather than later. It's already almost one."

"Really?" She glanced at her watch. In some

ways, it felt like it should be morning already. The hours had dragged by.

"Do you want me to wait and drive you home?" He folded her into a hug. "I'm happy for you and him. It's just going to take a hot minute to get used to."

She chuckled and hugged him back. "Thank you. That admission really had to hurt."

"Yeah, you have no idea how much." Brody broke the hug and nodded to the room. "He's waiting for you."

She beamed a smile at him and went to Ryker's door, stopping only to knock and peek her head inside. "Hey." He smiled and lifted his hand. There was still an IV, so she was careful when she took his and leaned past the silver guardrail to kiss him. "You can't do that again. I thought I was going to have a heart attack when I got the call."

"I'll keep that in mind." He smiled up at her. "You called my stepfather."

She winced. "Yeah, Mom and I thought if the situations were reversed, we'd want someone to call for us."

"For normal family dynamics, perhaps." Ryker closed his eyes. "We aren't the typical family."

"Your brothers came."

His eyes snapped open. "What?"

"Yeah, Xander, Elias, Dimitri, and Killian? They wanted to make sure you were okay. I told Xander that you'd probably call him tomorrow. I may have made a mistake." She winced again and dropped her head back, looking at the ceiling. "I told them you were a highly-decorated captain of JDET. I don't think they knew that."

Ryker chuffed a harsh breath. "They don't want to know what I do."

She ran her hand through his short hair. "I didn't get that just now. They seemed worried and I could tell they care."

Ryker gave her a weak smile before his eyes dropped again. "Okay. I'll agree to disagree."

She leaned down and kissed his lips again. "I'm going to go so you can rest. I'll be back in the morning."

"No, sleep in, get some rest, and bring me some lunch. I know you're exhausted."

"Well, I'm not sure I can stay away that long, but I won't set an alarm." She stared at him for a moment before she asked, "Can I bring you anything else?"

"God, yes. Jeans and a tee-shirt and socks. I feel

exposed in this damn thing." He picked at his hospital johnnie.

"Well, that's because it is about twenty sizes too small for you." She brought up the untied fabric from his good arm and tucked it under his shoulder. "Do you think they'll let you put a tee-shirt on?"

"Maybe. In the guest room closet there are some winter flannel button-ups. Bring me one of those? No, wait." he dropped his head back on the pillow. "I don't want you going to the house."

"Why?"

"Because they haven't caught the shooters. We don't know why they targeted me. If they are watching the house, they'll see you. I don't want them to have access to my personal life."

"Would they be watching the house?"

"It is one theory." He opened his eyes. "Promise me you won't go back to my house, please."

"Okay. I'll call Brody in the morning and see if one of your people can stop by and get those things for you. I'll probably have them bring my clothes with them since most of my good work clothes are in your closet."

"Funny how that happened," he chuckled.

"Yeah, matriculation through the months." She

swept her hand through his hair again, unable to stop herself from touching him, reassuring herself he was going to be okay.

"Maybe you should move in with me when we figure this situation is done." His words were sleepy.

She smiled at him. "You could convince me. Until then, why don't you stay with me?"

He hummed as she combed her fingers through his hair again. "I don't want to lead them to you."

"Then we are going to have problems. I'm not leaving you. If you're not staying with me, we are going somewhere else together."

"It isn't safe." He closed his eyes. Against the pallor of his skin, the dark circles under his eyes slashed a deep reminder of his recent surgery and the reason for it.

"Then, Captain Terrell, we are going to have to find a location that is safe. Someplace people wouldn't look for you." She cringed but said it anyway. "We can stay with my parents."

He opened one eye. "I'd rather not."

The relieved sigh came in a rush of air. "Oh, thank God."

He chuckled and patted her arm. "Don't worry,

babe. We'll come up with something. Tomorrow."
His eyes closed and his words drifted off.

She leaned down and kissed his forehead.
"Tomorrow. I love you."

He mumbled something unintelligible, and his
eyes didn't open. She smiled and stared at the man
she loved. *Thank God they had another tomorrow
together.*

CHAPTER 10

Ryker groaned as he sat down in the chair beside his bed. Rayburn and Watson had delivered street clothes first thing in the morning before they'd gone into the office. They also snuck him a cup of coffee the size of his head and a grease-bomb egg sandwich with enough bacon on the damn thing to give the entire hospital a heart attack. It was fucking fantastic. He had to wait for someone to unhook him from the damn IV before he made a trek to the bathroom and changed.

Damn, he'd sweat bullets exercising before, but this was a new level of exhaustion. He'd tugged one of his XXXL t-shirts over his head and shoved his good arm through the armhole. Getting the material down past his bad shoulder took almost five minutes of gentle tugging and stretching the fabric without pulling against the surgical site. Now, he was shaking like a kitten left outside in a freezing rainstorm and really wanted to crawl back up onto that bed and go to sleep. Fuck, it wrung him out.

"What are you doing?" The stocky nurse stopped in his doorway. The guy pointed to the bed. "You want help to get back into bed or are you going to pass out where you are?"

Ryker narrowed his eyes at the guy and gutted himself up into a standing position. He would not have his ass handed to him. It had been one hell of a long time since anyone talked down to him, and he would not allow it now either. "I needed to get out of that damn hospital gown."

"Well, bravo. What are you going to do when the doc wants to check that incision?" The guy folded back his blanket and sheet and moved the pillow out of his way in addition to making sure Ryker didn't face plant as he made his way to the bed.

He grunted. *Well, hell.* "I hadn't thought that far ahead. My focus was stopping my shit from dangling in the breeze, if you get my drift."

The nurse chuckled. "I got you. What we're

going to need to do is cut this shirt up the side. We can use safety pins to close the material and protect your modesty."

Ryker got into bed, carefully adjusted his position, and slowly dropped his head back on the pillow. "That will work. When is the doc coming by?"

"Rounds start at nine. Depends on how many patients he has, but..." The guy glanced up at the clock. "Probably within the next hour."

"What's the likelihood he'll spring me today?"

"That's up to him."

Ryker glanced at the guy. "Right. So, based on your past experience with surgeries like mine, and with me saying that I won't hold you to anything you say or tell anyone what you've said, when is he going to cut me loose?"

The guy chuckled. "Probably tomorrow if all that moving around hasn't messed with his stitch work. He gets peeved when patients don't listen to directions."

Ryker frowned. "Nobody told me I couldn't get dressed."

The man turned and stared at him. Ryker caught a good visual of his name tag. Carl. "Did you ask?"

He chuckled. "Nah, I'm more of an 'ask for forgiveness rather than permission' type of guy." He wasn't really, but Carl didn't need to know that.

"Right. Make that the day after tomorrow. I'm going to go raid a supply cart, grab a couple safety pins, and come back. If the doc sees that, he might not let you go home until next week." The man laughed hysterically at his own joke and left.

"I would never have guessed you were a comedian." Ryker popped his eyes open. Xander and Killian stood just outside his door. His body tensed. The last time he'd talked to Xander was almost four months ago. That conversation had lasted twenty seconds. "May we come in?"

He nodded and watched as his half-brothers shuffled into the room. Xander was, as usual, dressed in a three-piece suit. Killian wore work clothes, although the last time he'd heard, Killian's construction company was the largest in the tri-state area. He should be in a suit. All the Ganas brothers were successful.

"We stopped by last night."

Ryker cocked his head. "Why?" It wasn't like they were close.

"To make sure you were okay. Dad called me to let me know you were here."

"Really? Hoping I was dead or dying, no doubt." The bitterness dripped from his low words.

Xander shook his head. "The old man knows he was wrong. He just can't bring himself to apologize. He's old-country proud." The Greek heritage was strong in the Ganas family.

Ryker snorted. "The man accused me of being responsible for Mom's death." He'd screamed that message at the top of his lungs when Ryker tried to see his mother at the hospital morgue. They buried her on the estate. No one notified him of the service. No one—including his half-brothers.

Killian drew a sharp breath. "We never thought that."

"You never said otherwise." Ryker flung the words back at his brother. "And thanks for letting me know when you buried her."

"He said he told you. Afterward, he ranted about how you didn't care enough to show up. Hell, we were all mourning. Numb. But when two and two didn't add up, we reached out to you." Xander slipped his hands into his pockets as he spoke.

"Yeah, nice to know it took a year for you to realize I wasn't responsible for her accident," Ryker fired back.

He'd lost his mom. She was driving into the city to have lunch with *him* when an accident in front of her on the interstate caused her to swerve. She hit the retaining wall, and the car flipped into oncoming traffic. Thankfully, no one else suffered, but his mother's neck broke on impact. According to the highway patrol unit first on scene, she was dead when he arrived. But Benjamin, his stepfather, had fixated on the fact that she wouldn't have died if she hadn't been going to meet him. Her death became his fault because Benjamin had to have someone to blame and he was the easy target. Always the easy target.

Good ole Ben hated him. The man overlooked the fact his mother had a child out of wedlock, but that Ryker had the audacity to continue his relationship with his mother after Benjamin had asked him to leave the family estate when he was eighteen was unacceptable. Benjamin did everything he could to hinder Ryker from having anything to do with his brothers or his mother. At ten, Xander was the oldest when Ryker left. Killian was eight. He'd visit on the occasional holiday—when his mother's pleading had become too much for his stepfather—but Benjamin had never made him feel welcome, even though the vicious man loved his mom with a singular devotion.

"It took us a year to find you. I hired a private investigator." Xander shrugged. "We didn't know you'd changed your last name from Ganas."

Ryker smiled tightly. "Your father requested it. He told me he didn't want me to pollute the waters for *his* sons." The bastard had the audacity to offer to pay him off. As if. He took his mother's maiden name, the name he had before Ben adopted him. Another concession for his mother that Benjamin Ganas told him he regretted.

"Christ." Killian groaned and dropped into the chair Ryker'd just vacated. "He's a piece of work, isn't he?"

"I can think of other modifiers," Xander agreed. "Ryker, I'm not trying to make amends for him. Lord knows I can't. However, we'd like to get to know you again. When we were younger, you were our hero." Xander smiled. "You taught me to stand up for myself."

"And you helped build that birdhouse. You ignited my passion for building." Killian added. "And it was you that taught Dimitri to ride that damn mini-bike. He credits you for getting him into motocross."

"Another strike against me, according to Benjamin, no doubt," Ryker chuffed in response. Dimitri had been a champion motocross rider and catapulted that experience into launching a new federation of racing that was taking root worldwide.

"You were always there for us. Until he made you leave," Xander confirmed. "Mom tried to hide how sad she was when you left. But we could tell."

His nerves throbbed, exposed, bloody and raw. He'd shoved all the heart-wrenching emotions about his mother's death away, forcing them behind doors he'd never let his mind open again. The sudden appearance of his half-brothers and their admissions threatened to unlock those barriers.

"Why are you here?" He let his gaze travel first to Xander and then to Killian.

"Because I want to get to know my big brother again." Xander's voice was deep with emotion.

"I want that, too." Killian stood and shoved his hands in his jeans pockets. "And to tell you if you ever need anything not to go to cousin Andreas," Killian chuckled. "He was really butthurt the house he was flipping had bullet holes in it."

A surprised bark of laughter shot from Ryker.

"Well, let me tell you, that wasn't something we expected." He winced and leaned a bit to ease his shoulder.

"I hear from your girlfriend that you're a highly decorated officer." Xander smiled at him. "I'm not surprised. I always knew you'd be amazing at whatever you set your mind to do."

Ryker grunted. "I'm just a cop."

"A captain in charge of a highly-decorated, multi-jurisdictional drug enforcement team. I did a little research after Brianna told us about your commendations." Xander glanced at his watch. "And I need to go, I have a new client coming into town today." He placed his hand on Ryker's foot. "I mean it, Ry. We need you in our lives."

He nodded, the emotion tightening his throat, preventing any comment. Killian stood and moved beside Xander. "I'll go now, too. But I'll be back. Can I bring you lunch? Maybe a gyro from Aunt Tallie's?"

Ryker smiled at that. Aunt Tallie's was on the other side of the city. It had been Killian's favorite when he was little. The food would be a wet mess before Killian could get it here. "Nah, I'm good."

He watched his brothers leave and closed his

eyes. Not because they were leaking. No. He was just tired.

"All right. I have the scissors and the safety pins. And just in time, the doctor is next door." Carl, his nurse, buzzed in and grabbed the hem of his shirt. The razor-sharp scissors made quick work of the cotton from hem to armpit and the fabric opened. Carl dropped the scissors into his pocket and quickly attached two safety pins to the fabric under his sling-hobbled arm. "Next time, ask for help." Carl checked his watch. "You're due your meds soon. How's the pain?"

"Manageable if I don't move too much." Actually, he didn't hurt as much as he'd expected. It was the weakness after the surgery that was kicking his ass.

"That's good. Oh, here's the doctor." Carl turned and gave him a wide-eyed stare. The 'I saved your ass' look made him chuckle.

He dealt with the doctor's poking and prodding, took a pain pill, and dozed for a while. A knock brought him from a light sleep. Ryker sized up the big man. Broad shoulders, heavy muscles, and a short haircut. He didn't know this guy and, given the fact the man was wearing the duty uniform for Hope City Fire Department, the man probably had the wrong room. "Can I help you?"

"Yeah... no. I think I can help you, though." The guy crossed his arms. The shoulders and biceps on the guy were thick with corded muscle, but he didn't seem menacing, although the fixed stare could burn a hole through him.

Ryker arched an eyebrow. It was about as much energy as he had right now. "Exactly how do you plan on that? Am I on fire?"

The guy shook his head and then laughed. "Dude, I'm sorry. My name is Blay. I'm Brie's younger brother. Mom and Dad called last night. I understand you need a place to stay."

Ah, the eyes, yes, he could see the resemblance there, but unlike Brie and Brody, Blay's coloring was lighter and his facial features were stronger or perhaps more squared off. His mind caught up with the conversation. "Wait. They called you about me? Is that why you're here?"

"Nah, I'm here because one of our guys got his ankle tweaked when he fell through some floorboards at a house fire this morning. The rest of the team is two floors down." He adjusted the radio on his hip. "I can't be gone long, but I wanted to pop up and tell you I may have a solution for you."

"I didn't ask for help, but thank you." He was going to look for a place to stay today because Carl was right, the doc was making him stay one more night. He had time to figure something out.

Blay tipped his head back and laughed, his arms wrapped around his stomach. "Oh, man, you are so screwed. Mom already has your life arranged for the foreseeable future."

Ryker narrowed his eyes. "How?"

"Well, see, I've been renovating an apartment. I was going to move in next weekend. I've been couch surfing with Rory while I put the finishing touches on the place. She suggested that I offer you the apartment until they catch whoever has it out for you."

"You don't need to do that. I'm sure I can find a place."

The guy sobered quickly. "Dude, have you met my mom? It's either my apartment or their house. You want to use my apartment. Trust me."

"Yeah, again, I appreciate the offer, but your mom doesn't run my life." He was forty-six, damn near forty-seven years old. He could find his own place to stay.

The guy laughed again walking back to the door, HCFD sprawled in print across the back of his shirt. He stopped, shaking his head as he turned. "You have so much to learn." He braced his arm against the door jamb. "Got to tell you, I thought you'd be younger."

Ryker flew his middle finger at the guy, which earned him another laugh. "Oh, dude, I'm not criticizing. If you have the energy and the drive to keep up with Brie, you're okay in my book. Now Brock, he may be just a bit more miffed. You made him do math, man."

Ryker rubbed his face. What the hell was this guy talking about? Fuck, no more pain pills. He was having problems keeping up with this conversation. "Excuse me?"

He laughed again and shook his head. "You realize they figured out how old you'll be when you and Brie have kids, right?"

"Kids?" His voice strangled a bit. Kids? Who said anything about kids? Did he want kids? Well, yeah. Maybe. Probably.

"Yep. Anyway, the offer is there to use the apartment. It is a keyed entry building, oh, and your sergeant owns it. Cozy, that's what it would be. Mighty cozy, especially if Brie is going to stay with you."

"Yeah, thanks but no thanks."

"Think about it. It is better than the alternative. Besides, Rory is going to let me hang with him at his place. Actually, I'm teaching him how to lay flooring so I'm not wearing out my welcome."

That was the second time Brie's brother mentioned that name. Was that a relative, a brother she hadn't mentioned? "Rory?"

"McBride. Our next-door neighbors. Brie told you about the McBrides, right? Colm is retired CIA and Sean's a homicide detective. Tara McBride is married to Carter Fiske, he's a narcotics detective, then there's Kyle, also narcotics, but you should know those guys, seeing how you're the JDET Commander. Rory and I are the odd ones out. Rory is a paramedic and I'm HCFD, but hey, every family needs a non-conformist." He leaned his shoulder on the door jamb. "But seriously. You and Brie, that's cool, but don't make the mistake of thinking we won't hunt you down if you hurt our sister." The man winked at him and left.

Ryker dropped his head back onto the pillow. "Holy shit."

CHAPTER 11

Brie parked behind her restaurant with the phone wedged between her shoulder and her ear. "Mom, thanks again, but no, we aren't staying at the house with you and Dad. Ryker and I are looking for somewhere to stay today. I need to stop and make sure everyone is set at the restaurant before I head to the hospital."

"Have you talked to Blay? He will let Ryker take his apartment in Brody's building until all this blows over." Hannah King tsked and kept talking, "Rory needs help with his floors anyway."

She cut off the engine and leaned back in her seat. "That may work, but I'm going to ask Ryker before I agree to anything."

"It's the perfect solution. It is a keyed entry, and

there are two cops above him. He has instant backup. That was Dad's input, although I suggested keeping Gage here for the duration of Ryker's stay. Your dad thought it was a great idea."

Brie closed her eyes. "Thank you for the option, we'll discuss it." She knew her mother would try to convince her if she didn't give in and at least accept the possibility.

"Absolutely. Now, I have to run. Gage has a half-day today. I'm picking him up so Dawn doesn't have to take a half-day off work." Amber's stepsister and her mother had coordinated a schedule to pick up Gage after school. "Then we are going to Sharon's to bake with her and Colleen."

"Bake? Does Gage like to do that?"

"No, but he likes to eat the finished product, and he's good with Colleen. She idolizes him."

She glanced at her watch. The kitchen staff would be knee-deep in lunch prep. She had to make sure Roger had everything he needed. With the screw up in deliveries, he'd need the credit card from the safe and access to pending orders, which were on her computer. "He's a great kid, they both are. Listen, I've got to go, Mom. I love you, and I'll talk to Ryker."

"All right, honey. I'll talk to you tonight. Love you."

"I love you too, Mom." She hung up and dropped her cell into her purse. She'd taken the gun last night and placed it in her glove box, locking it in the vehicle while she was at the hospital. She glanced at the glove box and scrunched her nose. It was broad daylight. Those jerks were nowhere around. She cast a glance up and down the alley just to make sure. That camera system was still in her office. *Damn it.* Another thing she needed to add to the list of things to ask Roger to do. He needed a pay raise or at least a bonus for stepping up while she was with Ryker.

She jumped from her old SUV and locked it as the back door opened and Shane, the dishwasher, exited with two bags of garbage. "Hey, Boss. Your man okay?"

"He's going to be, thank goodness. Here, let me help you." She reached for one bag.

"Nah, I got this. Roger said you'd probably be taking a couple days off. Don't you worry about nothing, Brie, we'll all chip in and take care of everything. God knows you take care of us well enough." He propped the door open with his heel.

"Thank you, and if the city doesn't empty that

dumpster tomorrow, you may have to call them. The new guy driving the route has forgotten us twice."

"No worries. I'll keep an eye open." Shane let the door close behind her.

"Brie! How's Sexy Voice?" Roger shouted the question from across the kitchen, stilling every hand.

"He'll be okay." A collective sigh and hurried words preceded the rush to finish lunch prep. She nodded to Roger, who immediately started wiping his hands. They met at her office door and he opened it with her keys.

She flicked on the light and held her hand out for her keys. He dropped them into her palm. "I'm going to take some time off. There are a lot of unanswered questions about what happened last night."

"You take whatever time you need. We'll be fine. You've trained these guys, and more than that, they respect you. We'll make a go of it."

"Thank you. I needed to hear that." She rubbed her neck. "You'll need some information and access. Do you have time?"

"Sure. The prep is complete, and I've already

seasoned the pork tenderloins for tonight's special."

"Okay, well, on top of running the show, could you somehow manage to put that up above the back door?"

"What is it?"

"A camera system. Just hook it up to this computer system for now. I'll try to figure out the cloud stuff when I get back."

"You got it. What about passwords and such?"

Brie nodded to the chair. "Have a seat and grab a piece of paper. I need to be at the hospital by noon. Oh, can we get two specials to go?"

Roger made to stand and then hesitated. "He can eat non-hospital food?"

"It was his shoulder they shot, so probably. He told me to bring him lunch, so I'm going to do that." Her shoulders rode up to her ears when Roger bellowed the instructions from her doorway.

He sat down, crossed his legs, and picked up a pen before he tugged a piece of bond paper from the printer. "Okay, hit me with all the deets."

Brie chuckled and started detailing things that Roger would be responsible for during the next week. Two sheets of paper later, Roger shook his head. "How the hell do you do all of this *and* help us?"

"Organization, I guess." She stared at the open programs on her computer and the stacks of invoices on her desk. "I'll come in on Sunday and pay the bills."

"I can write the checks, so all you have to do is sign them." Roger stood. "Don't worry, I've got this. If I don't know what to do or can't figure it out with common sense, I'll call you."

"Thanks. I owe you."

"No, we all owe you." He walked her to the kitchen and snagged a white plastic bag that held their lunches. "Here, go see your man and let us worry about this place. I don't want to see or hear from you for a week."

She spun and pointed a finger in his face. "But you'll call if you have any problems, right?"

"Absolutely." He spun her and gently pushed her toward the door. "We'll take care of your baby. Go."

She drew a deep breath and looked back, searching the busy kitchen. Finally, she nodded. "Okay. Thank you." She gave him one more smile and pushed the heavy metal door open. The smell of today's special, steak quesadillas with rice and beans, filled her senses as she skipped down the stairs. The asphalt radiated the heat of the day back into the small confines of the alley. Brie shrugged her purse over her shoulder and rounded to the driver's side door.

The pain of her wrist being grabbed and twisted a fraction of a second before a hand clamped over her mouth immobilized her. On instinct, she screamed. "Shut your mouth, bitch, and maybe you'll live to see tomorrow."

No! Frozen to the spot, she felt the man's spittle land on her cheek. She panted as her eyes darted to the restaurant door, but there would be no help with lunch service in full swing. The man holding her wrenched her purse from her shoulder. The leather of the strap scraped the bend of her arm when she tried to stop the son of a bitch from taking it from her.

She narrowed her eyes as her panic-induced immobility receded because she knew what to do. Her brothers, her father, and all the hours of self-defense classes had primed her for this moment. She was still scared, but damn it, she wouldn't let these men touch her without a fight.

She struck out with her foot, catching the other bastard approaching from the front of the SUV in the kneecap. He dropped to the asphalt. The man behind her lurched when she bit his hand. He clung to her wrist and spun her. The side of her face exploded in pain. The blond moved closer and pushed her to the ground, kicking her in the back. The other used her SUV to push himself up. He grabbed her purse and plucked out the money she had in her wallet. "You'll pay for that, bitch." They both swung toward the opening of the alley. The blond crammed her money into his pocket and launched her wallet at her. She turned, and it missed her face but hit her shoulder. They skittered away like rats.

Brie groaned and sat up. A sudden cascade of tremors shook her body. *Oh, God. She'd fought back.* She swallowed hard and drew several short, panting gasps of air. She rubbed her wrist which was sore from where the man had gripped it. She flexed it back and forth before lifting her quivering hand to her cheek. The pain there wasn't going to abate anytime soon and when she touched the swollen cheek, shooting stingers radiated from the bruise. A sound down the alley shook her out of her stupor. She grabbed her wallet and her purse, picking up the comb, pens, lip gloss, and various receipts that she'd left in the bottom. A car rolled past her. From where she was, unless they were looking between the cars, no one would notice her, even at noon. *Get up before they come back.*

Carefully, she got up and searched the ground. The bastards had taken her food, too. *Great.* She half-laughed and half-cried. *Why in the hell would she notice that?* What was she going to do? She turned and stared at the back door of the restaurant. If she went back in, she'd have to explain what happened. *No, that would be a zoo.* It seemed she was their target, and she was leaving for a week. By then, Roger would have the camera installed.

When they saw the security system, they'd find easier pickings. Growing up with cops in the house, she knew most small-time criminals targeted people who were unsuspecting and unprotected. She straightened and rolled her shoulders. No, there were a hell of a lot more important things going on right now. Two punks mugging her didn't even come close to the top of the pile. She opened her SUV, got in, and locked the doors immediately.

She glanced at her face and winced. Damn it. Makeup would not cover that up. She started the vehicle and she made her way from the alley into the flow of traffic. She coasted through the drive-through lane of Famous Mike's Burger Barn and ordered Ryker a double-double stacked. Double cheese, double meat, with everything on top of it. Two orders of waffle-cut fries, a large soda for him, and a chocolate shake for her. She'd eat her fries and drink the shake on the way to the hospital.

She moved forward to pay for the order and a young woman leaned out of the window and pointed toward the side of her face. "Oh, that looks like it hurts. What did you do? Hit yourself in the face with the car door? I've done that before. Man, did I feel stupid. That will be twenty-three fifty."

Hell, that would work as an explanation, wouldn't it? She wasn't exactly accident prone, but she'd had her fair share of ungraceful moments. Twisting her ankle when she stepped off a curb, falling down a couple of steps when she wasn't paying attention. "Actually, yeah, I did."

"You want a cup of ice? You can hold it up against your face. Maybe it won't bruise too much."

"Thank you. That would be wonderful." She handed the woman her debit card, which the cashier swiped and handed back to her.

"No worries. Pull up to the next window." The woman shut her drive-through window and lowered her mic, taking the next order.

Brie collected her order and a large cup of ice. She'd eat at the hospital with Ryker instead of on the way. In the meantime, she pressed the thin cardboard against her cheek and prayed the ice held the swelling at bay.

"Hey, Cap." At Brody's greeting, Ryker opened his eyes. *Damn, he'd fallen asleep again, hadn't he?*

"Hey." He cleared his throat and glanced at the clock on the wall in his room. "Shit, those pain pills really kick my ass."

"Well, yeah. That and, you know, major blood loss and surgery." Brody grabbed one of the plastic chairs, spun it, and straddled it, his arms folded across the top of the chair. "I went to visit Mrs. Thorn this morning. She's quite the character. Makes damn good cookies." Brody smiled at him. "I had a bag full." He reached in his pocket and produced a baggie with crumbs in it. "Didn't quite make it here."

"You're an ass." Ryker chuckled and hit the

button on his bed to sit up higher.

"Yeah, but I'm a damn good detective." Brody arched an eyebrow.

Ryker stilled. "What did you find?"

"That SUV parked down the street. Three days in a row. It was on the far side of her camera, parked down by the row of townhomes. They watched you come home. After you went into the house, they drove forward. Two men. The footage is too grainy to get an ID without tech enhancing it. They parked directly in front of Mrs. Thorn's home and watched your house for about a half-hour, then they left."

"You watched the entire feed? They didn't come back later?"

Brody drew a breath. "You're worried they saw Brie come to your house after closing the restaurant?"

He nodded. Worried? Damn it, it terrified him. Protecting the woman he loved was the only thing that mattered.

"So was I. I watched that video three times. They showed up about the time you left the precinct and headed home." Brody rubbed his face. "Which means they were watching you and knew when you left work."

"I'm assuming you're pulling the feed for the precinct cameras?" Fucking hell, how had he not seen someone observing him?

"That's where the lieutenant is right now. Oh, and by the way, the commissioner's office announced the realignment of the JDET team during the morning media call. Seems we are out from under Fenton for good. And that is a good thing because after Brianna called him a dickless wonder, I don't think I could keep a straight face while talking to him."

Ryker chuckled. "She's a firecracker."

"Always has been." Brody cleared his throat. "She's my sister, Cap. Don't hurt her."

Ryker stared at his sergeant, and yes, his friend. "I'd kill myself before I purposely hurt her."

Brody stared at him for a second before he dipped his chin.

Ryker blinked back his emotion and searched for a less emotional topic. "Did you get a plate from the video?"

"I did. You'd be proud of me. I gave the video and the plate number to Callaway and Forsythe." Brody shrugged. "After I ran the plate, of course."

"Of course." Ryker shifted his arm to ease the tension in his shoulder. "Stolen?"

"Yep. Reported stolen last month," Brody confirmed his suspicion.

"Dead end." Ryker sighed. "It all comes back to Mouse, doesn't it?"

"I think so. We need to talk to Mouse."

Ryker shook his head. "She'll only talk to me, and she's in lockdown right now. Rehab."

"Well, that gives us some time. Forsythe told me they found Alice face down in the Cascade River. According to the report, she'd been floating for a couple days. It wasn't pretty. Even after being fish food, he said the coroner could tell they did a hell of a job on the poor girl." Brody shuddered. "I don't see how Brock can do that shit."

"You learn to separate yourself from it." Working for the living, not the dead. There was literally nothing he could do for a decedent, but he'd worked damn hard to find a murderer, and in doing so find closure for the family.

"Damn, that's right. You worked Homicide for a couple years, right?" Brody rubbed his chin.

"Seven years, until I promoted myself out of it. I called in favors to get Mouse to a rehab center in New York. I'll call and set up an appointment to go see her."

"You going to be up for that?" Brody nodded at his shoulder.

"I'll let someone else drive. I don't want to wait any longer. Mouse knows something, even if she doesn't know she knows it." He stared out the window at the brilliant blue sky.

Brody nodded. "Why would Peña act against a high ranking HCPD officer? He has to believe you have something of his."

Ryker swung his eyes toward Brody. "Mouse."
"What?"

"What if he thinks Mouse is his?"

"Cap, Mouse was a pro, right?"

He nodded. "But she said something. She said she and others were party favors, that's how she knew Peña and Rubio. What if Peña or Rubio decided Mouse was the flavor of the year?"

Brody nodded his head. "That would do it. If either of them is looking for what they consider their property and they thought you had Mouse, they'd steamroll you to make a point."

"Don't mess with cartel property." *Fuck, Mouse was terrified. If she'd been claimed as property, there was no telling the shit she'd endured. It was a miracle she'd escaped.*

"She's probably heard and seen a lot more than

what she admitted." Brody rubbed the back of his neck.

He nodded. "Yeah." He unlocked his phone and scrolled down through his call log until he found the New York number he needed and called it.

"Springside Rehabilitation Clinic, this is Andie."

"This is Captain Ryker Terrell, Hope City Police Department. I'm calling to check on a patient I dropped off recently. Sarah Mulligan. I'm on her form for release of information."

"One moment, Captain." They placed him on hold, the mind-numbing classical music interspersed with static.

Brody moved out of the way when an aid brought in his lunch. Ryker glanced at the tray and rolled his eyes. Brie was bringing him lunch. The crap on the tray was just going to sit there. Brody carried his chair to the other side of the bed, straddled it, and waited.

"Captain, thank you for holding. I had to validate you were on the information release forms. Due to HIPPA concerns we need to authenticate your identity. Would you please tell me the password you both decided on when she was dropped off?"

"Cottages." Ryker gave the password.

"Thank you, sir. Sarah is doing well. The notes indicated extreme exhaustion and depression, which isn't uncommon. She's progressing as expected. If you have any further questions, I can try to find one of the doctors."

"I have one question. If she chose to check herself out, could she?"

"Yes, sir. She's a voluntary admit. We couldn't hold her. Why? Do you believe she'd want to leave?"

"No, as a matter of fact, I think she'll stay as long as possible." Mouse was smart—she'd probably figured out as long as she wasn't on Peña's scope, she was safe. "However, I need to talk with her. I'll be coming down next week. What do I need to do to make that happen?"

"Normally, sir, we discourage visitation for the first thirty days."

"I understand that, but she is a witness in a case we are working, and we need to speak with her. It is a life and death situation." Hers and his. *Obviously.*

"Well, I can leave a message for Doctor Missolli. He must approve the visit."

"Please do that, and give him my number if he has questions." He rattled off his cell number and then gave them the number at the office just in case he didn't answer. Brody gave him a thumbs up, acknowledging the secondary number.

He hung up and dropped his phone to his lap. Brody shifted and leaned forward. "We aren't giving this information to Callaway and Forsythe, are we?"

"No. She's a witness who has information on an ongoing case JDET is working against Peña and Rubio. If we get other intel that specifically supports the assumption that Rubio and Peña are behind the attempted hit on me, we'll make the call to share information at that time."

Brody dipped his chin in acknowledgment. "We got the preliminary on the three bodies from the fire the other night. Desoto was an easy match as we suspected he was one of the victims. The ME confirmed him through his dental records. No ID's on the other two as of yet."

Ryker felt his gut drop. "Those fuckers need to be taken down."

Brody's attention riveted outside the open door. "What the--"

"What? What do you see?" He tightened his stomach muscles and sat up.

"Brie." Brody was up and moving.

"Fuck. What?" He swung his legs out of the bed before he saw her.

She held a white plastic bag. "I brought lunch." There was a red welt across her cheek and a puffy eye with a dark ring forming under it.

"What the fuck happened to you?" Ryker and Brody spoke at the same time.

She sighed heavily and set the takeout beside his hospital-supplied tray of food. "This is embarrassing. I had my purse and the lunch that Roger prepped for us, and I was trying to open the door to the SUV, and somehow, I got tangled up and popped myself with the door." She pointed to the burger bag. "Our lunch disappeared in that little tussle. So, you'll have to settle for a double-double."

Ryker reached for her with his good arm, and when she took his hand, he tugged her to where he sat, moving her between his legs. She bit her lip and flinched a bit as he reached up to push back her hair so he could see the extent of the damage. He narrowed his eyes. "How hard did you hit the door? Can you see okay?"

"I clocked myself, that's for sure, and yes, I can see fine."

"No headache?"

"No." She leaned forward. "But you can kiss it better for me."

"And with that, I'm out of here." Brody gave an exaggerated full-body shudder. "Never going to get that image out of my mind." He winked at them both before he left.

"Are you sure you're okay?" He carefully ran his finger across the tender skin of her cheek.

"I am. You don't need to worry about me. I can handle things myself." She spun and reached for the bag she'd brought in.

"What?" He placed his hand on her arm. "Babe, why would you say something like that?" She hesitated for a moment before she turned to meet his gaze.

Brie sighed and shook her head. "I'm just embarrassed. You have so much on your plate already." She made a motion to her face. "You don't need to worry about things like this."

He shook his head and wrapped his arm around her waist, pulling her closer. "Wrong. You will always be my first priority. Always." He leaned forward and winced a bit before she leaned in and met his lips. They moved apart but didn't separate. "I love you." He whispered the words against her lips.

She leaned forward and pressed a soft kiss against his lips. "I love you, too." She leaned back and nodded toward the bag. He noticed the wince at the action, but she turned away and asked, "Hungry?"

"I could eat." He nodded to the tiny table by the window. "Let's sit there. I'm tired of being in bed. Are you sure you're okay?"

"You haven't even been in bed twenty-four hours, and I'll be fine." She was at his side as soon as he stood.

He held the hand she offered, noticing the way it shook. "You're trembling."

"I haven't eaten anything, and I've had a pot or twenty of coffee. You're shaking, too."

He chuckled. "I got dressed this morning and thought I'd run a marathon. Wiped me out." He sat down and adjusted his position so he could face the table. "I slept most of the morning."

She retrieved a massive burger and two large orders of waffle fries. "What did the doctor say?"

"He wants an x-ray this afternoon and then, if everything is good, he'll release me tomorrow morning."

Brie unwrapped his burger and poured his fries onto the wrapper. She shook down a ketchup packet and opened it, squirting the contents onto the wrapper so he could dip his fries. Her hand still trembled.

"You're sure you're okay?"

"What? Yeah. Mom called this morning."

He took a drink of the massive, ice-cold soda and watched her, waiting for her to tell him what was actually happening. He'd been a cop for far too long not to trust his gut. Something else was going on, something she wasn't telling him. Brie cleared her throat. "She and Dad think it would be a good idea if you moved into Blay's apartment until you figure out what happened last night."

She tore her fry in half and nibbled on the damn thing. He could tell she was in pain, but she was trying not to show it. He dipped a fry into the ketchup and ate it before he responded. "First, we know what happened last night. Someone was trying to kill me. I will not put others at risk. What happened to you?"

Brie leaned back in the small chair and stared at him. "I told you, and we'll have to figure something out because you aren't getting rid of me. Brody and Amber have guns."

"And what about their kid?" Ryker picked up his burger with one hand and took a massive bite.

He wasn't ready to give up on what really happened to her, but he'd reattack that later.

"Oh, like Mom wouldn't love to have a reason to have Gage at the house." Brie picked up her shake.

"I met him today, you know," Ryker spoke around his food.

"Gage?" Brie's eyebrows popped toward heaven.

"Blay. He was here this morning. Offered me the apartment temporarily." He dipped another fry.

"He's a good kid." Brie nibbled on a fry. "It isn't a *bad* idea."

"The person I met today was a full-grown man, and it isn't the *best* idea either." Ryker shook his head. "I can get a room at a hotel."

"Wouldn't that put you at risk?"

"I don't think so. I believe the people who shot at me were sending a message." He leaned back and took a drink of his soda.

"So, us moving into a full apartment where I can cook us meals and take care of you is less preferable than us moving into a hotel room and having access to nothing." She nodded her head. "Got it."

"Manipulation." He picked up the burger again.

"Doesn't work on me." He took a bite and sat it down, wiping his chin with one of the paper-thin napkins that were in the bag.

"I don't like the idea of a hotel." She grabbed another fry and tore it into pieces, not really eating it. "Brody and Amber can load the apartment with food and bring our clothes from the house. You'd be able to heal, and I could hide for the next week with you. Roger has everything he needs, and he said he'd call if he ran into problems."

A wave of exhaustion rolled through him. As much as he hated to admit it, hiding for a week sounded like a fantastic idea. Minus the day he'd have to travel to New York, it sounded perfect. "Okay, but make sure Blay isn't doing this against his will."

"Oh, I guarantee Mom probably guilted him into it, but welcome to our world." Brie chuckled. "If you can't think of something better by tonight, we'll accept. And a hotel room is not a better idea, by the way." She pointed the straw of her drink at him as she spoke.

He nodded and closed his eyes. "My brothers stopped by this morning."

She cocked her head at him. "All of them? That's kinda sweet."

More like bittersweet. "No, just Xander and Killian. We worked through a few things."

"And these things you worked through involve..." She let the sentence go, asking for information she had every right to know.

"Our mother. Their father. A past that isn't pretty but not their fault—nor mine." He looked at his half-eaten burger and fries. "I think I'll save this for later. I'm tired."

Brie was on her feet and at his side immediately. At least she wasn't shaking when she helped him stand and make his way back to his bed. He'd just laid down when a nurse swooped in to take his vitals again and give him another pain pill. Brie put their lunch back into the bag and moved the chair to sit beside him. "You don't have to stay." He smiled at her surprised look.

"I know, but I want to. I have a book on my phone app that I want to read and being near you makes me feel... safer." She gave him a sad smile and winced. "I'm sorry for being clingy."

"I feel better with you here, too. You're not clingy." He closed his eyes. Her warm hand covered his, and he sighed. He felt so much better with her by his side.

CHAPTER 12

Well, hell. The apartment *was* way better than a hotel room. Brianna picked him up from the West Entrance, just in case someone was watching the hospital. He would not parade out the main patient entrance and wave a fucking flag in their face. Additionally, he wore a Hope City Captains cap tugged down, obscuring any direct recognition. Was it overkill? Probably, but for Brie's safety, yeah, he'd go the extra mile.

"Do you want to lie down?" Brie asked as she engaged the second deadbolt.

"God, no. I want a hot shower."

"Doc said not to get those stitches wet." Brie smiled at him. "Blay has an amazing bathtub."

He groaned. "Babe, I am so not a bathtub type of guy."

She smiled and started walking backward through the living room that boasted floor-to-ceiling views of the harbor. "Did I mention the tub is big enough for both of us?"

Ryker smiled and started after her. "No ma'am, you did not." The puffiness that had dominated her cheek and eye yesterday had receded. Makeup mostly covered the black under her eye.

"No?" She reached down and grabbed the hem of her shirt and pulled it over her head. The leopard print bra was new. She popped the top button of her slacks. "I could have sworn I mentioned it. Olympic-sized. With jets." She kicked off one heel and then the other, backing away from him as he moved forward.

She shimmied from her slacks at the end of the hall she was leading him down.

"I'm starting to see the benefits of taking a bath."

"Right? We need to loosen all those miserably tight muscles."

His woman turned, and he groaned. That leopard print thong framed her beautiful ass. His body was fully on board with this bath thing, especially as the doc hadn't put any limitations on him other than the obvious no lifting bullshit. Yeah, his muscle was tight and getting tighter behind sweats.

"I'm going to turn on the water and then I'll come back and help you with that problem that has popped up." She gave a low throaty laugh that did nothing to help the problem and everything to exacerbate it.

He followed her into a black marble haven. The shower took up one corner of the room. He gazed longingly at the array of showerheads that begged him to ignore the doctor's advice and step under them. He followed Brianna around the corner. "That is not a tub. That's a freaking jacuzzi."

"He installed extra vents to prevent the moisture from causing problems and reinforced the floor studs." Brie laughed. "I heard about this project every Sunday for months."

"Your brother has a *freaking jacuzzi* in his bathroom." A four-seat jacuzzi with steps and shelves installed around the thing, Blay'd mounted a TV in the nook's corner, exactly where any man would mount a sixty-five-inch television. "I may never leave." Ryker did a three-hundred-sixty-degree turn. "Damn, your brother is a genius."

Brie slid the bra straps off her shoulders and

reached behind her, freeing her full breasts. Damn, he'd never tire of looking at her. Those soft, feminine curves beckoned him closer. She shimmied out of the thong and met him halfway.

"Let's get you out of this." She kissed him until he groaned in urgency. With a sexy chuckle, she worked the safety pins, releasing his t-shirt, and then carefully helped him remove the material. The sling went next. He was careful to keep his arm tucked close to his body. Brie reached past him to one of the shelves. She peeled a clear plastic sheet off its backing and carefully placed it over the bandage already on the surgical incision. "This is going to pull your chest hair when we take it off." She smoothed the sticky material onto his skin. "But it will keep your stitches dry and still allow you to relax."

"You were planning on this?" He nodded to the jacuzzi.

"Since the moment you told me we could stay here. I asked the nurses what I could use to protect your surgical site. They got me several of these sheets. The PTs use them when they do hydrotherapy for knee replacements and such." Her hands smoothed down his chest, past his arm that laid uselessly at his side and down to his waistband. She tugged the sweats and bent down with the effort. Her breath against his cock damn near made him pass out. He reached down with his good hand and threaded his fingers through her hair. She tapped his foot, and he lifted it. She repeated the process on the other side.

Brie cupped his erection and licked a hot, wet stripe up the underside of his cock. Fuck, yeah, her mouth was so damn good against him. She stood up and extended her hand. "Come with me."

To the ends of the earth and beyond. All she had to do was ask, and he'd follow her anywhere. She got into the jacuzzi first and steadied him as he found his footing.

"I lowered the temperature last night. The nurses said not to make it too hot, but it's warm enough to be comfortable."

He leaned back against the molded seatback and fuck him if he didn't feel like crying. The heat and the gentle movement of the jets were exactly what he needed. "Fuck, babe. This is perfect." He swallowed hard and let his head fall back.

"No, not yet it isn't." She cupped his shaft, which popped his eyes open. Brie chuckled. "Shhh. You just sit there and enjoy. Doctor Brie's orders." She rolled to her side, perching her hip against a small molded ledge and freeing both hands. She kissed his good shoulder as she moved closer. "Just relax." One hand cupped his balls, the other worked his shaft. Her tongue licked the rim of his ear and then funneled inside his ear in the same rhythm of her hand.

He shuddered and tightened his abs against a too-quick onslaught. "Babe, so good." His head lolled against the seatback as he surrendered to her touch. Her fingers rolled his balls, giving them a small tug when she tightened her hand and squeezed the head of his cock. He grabbed her leg with his good arm, looking for something, anything, to ground him to her. She bit his earlobe, and that was it. His back arched against his orgasm. A zing of pain lanced from his shoulder to his fingertips as he came in her hand.

He reached for her after she removed the wash-cloth in which she'd captured his release. "Let me make you feel good."

"You make me feel good just by being here beside me." She held herself away from him. He could tell she was afraid she'd hurt him.

"Not the same thing." He wanted to give her pleasure, to make her lose her mind and forget about the stress she was under, too.

"I don't think it's a good idea. I can wait until those stitches are out." She licked up the column of his neck to his ear and whispered, "But when those stitches are gone, I'm going to ride you like a bucking bronco."

He knew his woman. "Think you can last that long?"

"One hundred percent, Mr. Terrell."

Brie braced herself, her arms against the headboard as Ryker slid into her from behind. She'd resisted his advances for two-and-a-half days. But today, he wanted her, and damn it, she needed him. His big hand held her hip as he eased out and then back in. His hot, hard cock electrified every nerve ending in her body. A ripple of sensation shimmered across her skin. She leaned back as he thrust forward. The slow, languid way he was taking her was the reason her insides rippled, tightened, and sizzled. She threw her head back and gasped as she came. Her body seized around him as waves of pleasure engulfed her. She felt him climax and allowed herself to lower to her elbows.

Panting to regain her breath, she reached around and grabbed his thigh. "You... okay?"

He rubbed her hip with his hand. "Yeah... Perfect... You?" He was breathless too.

"No. I'm kicking myself for not doing that sooner." He moved away, and she flopped to the side. He dropped to his heels. God, what a sight he was. Sweaty from making love to her, he glistened.

She snorted and then laughed. At least he didn't sparkle.

Ryker cocked his head and glared at her. "Laughing after sex should be a communal thing. Otherwise, one of us is likely to get a complex."

She laughed harder and forced herself to crawl to where he sat. "I was laughing, but not at you. A joke that isn't funny unless you've read vampire romance novels."

He put his hand under her chin and dropped a kiss on her lips. "Sorry, never indulged."

"Too bad. The sparkle joke was pretty--" A resounding knock at the front door stopped her response.

"What the hell?" She scrambled from the bed and threw on a robe.

"Don't open the door without finding out who it is." Ryker's shout followed her down the hall.

"I'm not two!"

His, "Thank God," reply made her snort another laugh.

"Who is it?" She sang the question loudly as she neared the door.

"Brie, it's Brody. Have you checked your phone?"

She frowned and unlocked the locks, opening the door enough to see her brother. "Not lately. Why?"

He glanced down at her robe and rolled his eyes. "The horde is about to descend on you. I've diverted them to my place, but everyone and the McBrides are coming for Sunday dinner in about thirty minutes." Brody waved at her robe. "You two need to get presentable and come upstairs."

"What? Dinner isn't until six!"

"They want to visit." Brody gave her a fake-ass smile. "I'm heading to the store for beer and wine. Get upstairs and help Amber, will ya?"

"Yeah, of course. I just need to…"

Brody groaned and turned away. "I don't want to know. Not ever." He headed down the stairs. "Do you hear me? Never!"

She shut the door and fell against it. "Damn it."

"What?"

"We are having a family event."

"When?"

"Thirty minutes. Upstairs. The entire troop is descending."

"Oh. Okay. I need to clean up." Ryker turned and headed down the hall.

"Wait, aren't you intimidated in the slightest?" She jogged across the plush carpet of the living room after him.

He stopped and turned. "Not in the slightest. I know most of them, and I'd like to meet your family."

"But it's not just my family. The McBrides are coming, too."

"Babe, are you worried they won't like me?" Ryker tugged her to him, carefully tucking her against his good shoulder. He kissed her hair and held her tightly.

"No. I guess I just don't want *you* to not like *them*."

"Babe, they're important to you. I'll like them. Now, let's get cleaned up and get upstairs."

CHAPTER 13

"Stop staring. He's a big boy, he'll be all right," Tara McBride whispered as they put together a tray of finger foods from the hodgepodge of potluck dishes that had been streaming in the door for the last ten minutes.

"Was it this hard when Carter met your family?" She glanced up again, finding Ryker across the room talking to Brock and Brody. From the frowns on all of their faces, the conversation wasn't pleasant. A tingle of apprehension zipped through her. "Oh, shoot. Should I interrupt?"

"No, look." Tara nodded as the three men sought out her father, who was talking to Colm McBride. "It is probably business. Not a family issue."

Her father's smile diminished, and he folded his arms, focusing intently. He nodded his head and his eyebrows drew together. She agreed with Tara, "Yeah, looks like business."

"He is gorgeous, Brie." Tara bumped her with her hip and smiled.

Brie checked to make sure they were alone before she returned her friend's smile. "I never imagined I could fall in love in three months' time, but Tara, I'm lost. He is so wonderful."

"When you meet the right man, you just know it. That was the way it was for me and Carter." Tara grabbed one of the open wine bottles and motioned for her to swipe a couple of stemless wine glasses. She held them as Tara filled them. "So, fill in the details. I haven't seen or talked to you in almost two months. We have to make time for each other."

They moved into a corner by the front door, just a few feet away from the kitchen in case someone needed them, but Sharon and her mother were in their element, arranging and organizing. "Right? You're busy with your family and I've been spending all my time with Ryker."

"How are you managing that? Hover Mother letting one of her birds fly the coop?"

Tara giggled when she rolled her eyes. "Mom is blessedly busy with Gage. But seriously, she's been very supportive of my relationship with Ryker, even if my brother had a cow or twenty."

"What? Who? You mean more than the normal macho positioning?" Tara swung her gaze past her and swept the room, her eyes landing on her husband. As if he knew she was looking, Carter turned in her direction and smiled back at her. A tinge of a blush rose to Tara's face.

"Brody. He had a tantrum and had the audacity to bring up Ryker's age. As if that was any of his business."

"Why how much older is he?" Tara lifted her wineglass to her lips.

"Almost fourteen years."

Tara's eyes popped, and she immediately looked at Ryker. "No way."

"Way. He'll be forty-seven soon." Brie took a drink of her wine.

"Girl, every woman in America wants her husband to be that buff when he turns forty-seven." Tara shook her head. "Tell Brody to shove off."

"Oh, she did." Amber and Kallie strolled from the kitchen. Amber held a glass of wine; Kallie carried her usual—bourbon, neat. Amber chuckled, "He was a little full of himself for a while. I think he was more concerned with what the relationship would do to his and Ryker's work association more than Brie and the Captain actually being together."

"He doesn't seem to have any problem now." Kallie nodded toward the men. Carter, Sean, and Kyle had joined the conversation, but the topic must have changed because there was laughter from the huddle.

"Where are Rory and Blay?" Harper drifted from the kitchen with Erin and Caitlyn.

"And Bekki?" Caitlyn craned her neck around. "She was here a minute ago."

"I'm here!" Bekki practically bounced out of the kitchen with a bottle of spring water in her hand.

"Oh, good. Excuse us, please." Brie grabbed her wrist. "We need to have a conversation." She hauled Bekki down the hall.

Bekki laughed and tried to grump, "What? I did nothing, I swear!"

"No, but you will." Brie pushed her into the bathroom. "I need you to do something for me, and you can't tell a soul where you got the information or Ryker will go through the roof."

Bekki's face lost all traces of humor. "What's up?"

Brie drew a deep breath and detailed her conversation with Councilman Davis.

Bekki's brows drew together. "I've been looking into other areas of graft within the city government and Councilman Davis' name has come up more than once. Has anything strange happened? Anything at all?"

"Again, you can't tell a soul." She waited for Bekki to agree. "There were orders that suddenly vendors can't fill and…"

"And? Come on, don't keep me hanging."

"Well, I don't know if it's related, but I've had my tire slashed and there are two guys that have been strong-arming me for money."

Bekki grabbed her arm. "Oh my God, Brie! Have you filed a police report? Have you told anyone?"

"No, but I've bought a security system and Roger is having it installed while I'm taking time off. I know if those two punks see there is a system recording them, they'll move on. They are low-level scum. I don't need to run to Dad—or Ryker, for that matter."

"I don't like it, Brie. You need to make sure the

police are aware of what those guys are doing." Bekki shook her head and stared past her to the wall. "If I could tie the vendors that cancelled their orders to Councilman Davis, it could be the leverage I need to convince the station this is a story they should allow me to follow."

"I wish you well. That man is slimy. He has a great public façade, but let me tell you, he's a snake." Brie shuddered.

Bekki stood and nodded. "I'll look into it under one condition."

Brie knew her sister—tit for tat was Bekki's wheelhouse. "What's that?"

"If those two scumbags show their faces again, you will call the cops and tell them everything. No one else needs to know, but the local precinct needs to have a record of it." Her sister leveled her with a determined stare.

"Deal. I was going to report them if they showed again. They need to spend some time behind bars." She hugged her sister. "Thank you for taking this up."

"Thank you for the lead. If I can tie the graft from Councilman Davis to the particular organization within the city government that I've been investigating, it will make one hell of an exposé."

Bekki smiled widely. "It may even catapult me into the New York market."

"Well, then, I hope you find all the dirt on that scum." Brie opened the door and froze.

"What is going on?" Hannah stood outside the bathroom door.

"Nothing," both Brie and Bekki said at the same time.

"Really?"

"Okay, Mom, you caught us. We were discussing my total lack of boyfriends and I was asking Brie how her sex life was now that she had a stud like Ryker." Bekki crossed her arms and cocked her head. "Do you want to know what she said?"

Hannah's eyes peeled open wide. "I do not. Really, Bekki." Her mother shook her head. "Sometimes you take things a step too far."

"That's exactly what I said, Mom. Come on, let's go visit." Brie grabbed her mom's arm and gave Bekki a 'What the hell were you thinking' look. Bekki smiled wildly and winked. The girl would end up giving their mom a heart attack. It was just a matter of time.

Ryker watched Brie, her mother, and her younger sister meander back into the living room. Bekki was nothing like Brie. Brie was like a breath of fresh cool air; her sister was a hurricane-force wind. Whoever took that woman on would need infinite patience and a strong will. Brie's eyes bounced across the room until she saw where he was sitting. She smiled at him and he felt a warm smile spread across his face. He loved that woman more than life itself.

"Don't you agree, Cap?" Brody's question brought him back to the conversation.

He wasn't going to front. "I have no idea what you just said."

Carter Fiske chuckled. "Distracted, sir?"

"Ryker." He corrected and motioned around the room. "When we are with family, it's Ryker."

"Roger that." Carter lifted his bottle of beer in his direction.

"But to answer your question, yes, pleasantly distracted." He sent another look in Brie's direction.

"You know, I don't think I've had my little talk with you yet." Brock leaned back in his chair and brought his size thirteen boot over his knee. He leveled a glare at Ryker. It was easy to see why

Brock was good at investigations—he could intimidate, but Ryker had spent more years in the trenches than anyone in the room except for the Commissioner and Colm McBride.

"Neither have we." Sean motioned between himself and Kyle.

Carter snorted. "Really guys? Do you honestly think that BS intimidation tactic is going to work on Captain... err, Ryker?"

Ryker nodded in Carter's direction, acknowledging the man's correction, but turned his attention back to the three men across from him. He leaned back, still holding his warm beer in his good hand. "Go ahead. No, wait. Let me guess. You'll string me up by the balls if I hurt your friend and sister. I can take on one of you, but not all of you. I'll be sorry I ever took a breath around her and I'll regret the day I was born." He took a drink of his beer as the men looked at each other. Brock started laughing, followed by the rest of Brianna's white knights.

Brody leaned forward and stared at him. "Cap, can we steal those lines? I mean, we still have Bekki, Erin, and Caitlyn to protect. They are a hell of a lot better than the ones we think up on the spur of the moment."

Ryker laughed and elevated his three-quarter full beer. "Be my guest."

"Better yet, let's take him with us." Kyle motioned in his direction. "Just get your wing healed up first. Because you don't look like you could do much to pound down the unworthy right now."

"Not true." Brody pointed at his boss. "He has like nine or ten black belts and is all ninja and shit."

"No way. What discipline?" Rory and Blay moved up chairs and sat down.

"I only have one black belt." He gave Brody a look and all the guys around the informal circle laughed.

"Right, which is one more than all of us put together." Blay leaned forward. "Seriously, what discipline do you study?"

"Muay Thai and Jiu Jitsu. The belt is in Jiu Jitsu." He'd started both classes at eighteen when he'd started living alone in the city. The discipline helped him curb his anger and his teachers had become father figures in a way his stepfather never was.

"You ought to see him fight. As big as he is, he's faster than anyone else in the ring." Brody laughed and leaned back. "No one wants to get into the ring with the Cap."

"That must be part of that 'Don't get dead' advice you ladle out." Sean McBride laughed, and when prompted by Kyle and Brock told the story of Ryker's advice for making captain.

"Hey, it's solid and smart." He chuckled and then grimaced when he took a swig of his warm beer.

"Need a new one?" Rory McBride stood up and five empties plus Ryker's warm brew pushed toward him. "Assholes." Rory grabbed three and Blay grabbed the others.

"Bring back snacks!" Brock yelled after them.

"No snacks. We're just about ready to eat," Hannah King called back. "As a matter of fact, everyone come into the kitchen."

Without even questioning her directive, Ryker stood up as did the other men. When he'd met Hannah earlier, he'd seen the love she had for her daughter. Her whispered, "I'm so happy to finally meet you," brought a stab of pain that his mother would never say the same to Brianna. He thanked her and greeted Chauncey before he was introduced and reintroduced to friends and family. The two youngsters, Colleen and Gage, waved and ran off to Gage's bedroom with a new movie to watch while the grown-ups visited. As the crew continued to arrive, he wondered if he could escape and watch a movie with them. But the afternoon's impromptu visit turned out to be pleasant, and he liked Brie's family.

"Everyone pipe down." Chauncey's voice rang above the laughter and talk. Ryker eased over to stand beside Brie, pulling her into his good side. She fit perfectly in his arms and in his life. "Today, we are officially meeting Brianna's man. I've known Ryker for a long time. If I had to pick someone for my daughter, he is exactly what I would look for. His integrity and professionalism aside, he takes care of his people, protects them, and gives them the support to do the job he hired them to do. Son, you take care of my girl like that and I will be a happy man."

"Thank you, sir." He looked down at Brie and kissed her. There were catcalls and boisterous laughter.

"Knock it off," Colm McBride commanded, and the din lowered. "Bow your heads." Collectively, the family did as the man ordered. "Lord, we thank you for the people who gather here today. Family. Plain and simple, by birth and by choice. We ask for your continued blessings on us and blessings on this food for the nourishment of our bodies in the service of you. Amen."

They formed a line and grabbed plates from the counter. Chauncey and Hannah, Colm and Sharon went first, helping the kids as they moved. They encouraged Ryker and Brie to go through the makeshift buffet next. He held his plate as Brie ladled food on it for him. She collected two napkin rolls with silverware in them and led him to one of the many card tables set up for the event.

"Kind of overwhelming, isn't it?" She unrolled the silverware and smiled at Gage and Colleen, who sat down with them. "Hey, kiddos. How was the movie?"

"It was good."

Gage spoke and Colleen nodded her head up and down, rapidly agreeing, "Superheroes. Gage likes superheroes."

"I do. Are we going to play football today?" the little boy asked and looked at him, or rather, his sling. "You probably shouldn't play even though it's just touch football."

Ryker gave the boy a serious look. "I think you are right. I may have to sit this one out."

Gage nodded, just as serious. "Accidents can happen."

"Can I play, Gage?" Colleen stared adoringly at the older boy.

"Sure, but you have to be careful not to get knocked down. I'll help you." He glanced around and then lowered his voice. "Don't play with Aunt Bekki. She's not very good."

"I heard that, Squirt!" Bekki yelled from two tables away where she was sitting with Amber's sister, Dawn, Blay, and Rory. "Just for that, you're on my team."

Gage craned his neck around and pleaded, "Daaad!"

Brody almost choked laughing. "Don't worry, I'll save you. You're on my team. We'll make Bekki the kicker."

Colleen tugged on Gage's arm and looked terribly concerned. "But the kicker never gets in the game."

"Exactly," everyone spoke at the same time, and laughter rolled through the room.

The joy and easy dynamics of the massive 'family' were something Ryker had longed for his entire life. Brie gripped his hand, and he turned to see her smile up at him. She knew. Her love shone like a beacon from her beautiful blue eyes. He smiled back and hoped his mother could witness this moment. He'd finally found his home with Brie.

"How is your shoulder?" Hannah King walked up beside him, drawing his eyes away from the game of football that was taking place across the street.

"Stiff." He smiled at Brie's mother briefly.

"I can imagine. May I ask you a question?" Hanna kept her eyes on the game, so he did too, although in his peripheral vision he could see her chew on her bottom lip nervously.

He really didn't want to open a can of worms, but the woman had a right to ask her questions and settle her mind about his and Brie's relationship. "Of course."

"What happened between you and your family?" Hanna hurried to add, "The reason I ask is that I've made mistakes. I think of the things I should have done differently, and I've wished I could see things from a fresh perspective. They call me Hover Mother." She chuckled and glanced at him.

Ryker smiled and continued to stare through

the window at the huge gathering now pretending to chase Colleen down the impromptu football field. Gage was running right beside her, encouraging her to go faster. "My mom got pregnant with me and her boyfriend bailed. We survived until she met Benjamin Ganas. He is a very proud Greek man with money. They fell in love and got married." He sighed. "He never accepted me. I was not his child and he never let me forget that, especially when Mom gave him four sons of his own. He asked me to leave when I turned eighteen."

Hannah gasped. "Surely, your mother didn't allow that!"

"No, she was livid, but honestly, I was ready to leave. I really loved the boys and Mom, but Benjamin made life at the house miserable. I carved a life for myself. Visited on holidays and Mom and I stayed close. She came into the city two or three times a month and we'd have lunch or go to dinner. She died that way. Coming into the city to see me. There was a car accident."

"Oh, my dear boy." Hannah leaned into him and he felt her hand rubbing his back.

A flash of his mother doing the same thing lanced through him. He let the emotion roll through him and continued, "Benjamin blamed me, of course. She wouldn't have been where she was when she was if she wasn't coming to see me. Which is true." He shrugged. He couldn't dispute that fact.

"You cannot believe her death is your fault." Hannah stared up at him.

"No, the accident wasn't my fault, but Benjamin used it as another wedge between the relationship I had with my brothers. We've been estranged since she died." His words faded as a whisper.

"Do they know the actual story?"

He realized Hannah's hand still rubbed his back. What should have been awkward wasn't. Instead, her care and support were comforting and... welcomed. "I believe so. After Brie called Benjamin, he let Xander know I was in the hospital. Why Ben did that, I'll never know, but Xander called the clan and they showed up at the hospital and met Brie. Xander and Killian showed up again the next morning. We had a conversation. It's a start."

Hannah nodded. "Beginnings after miscommunication and hurt are difficult. Believe me, I know. Been there, done that, and got the grandson."

He chuffed a breath of laughter. "I feel there is a story there."

"There most certainly is, but we'll leave that for another time." She pointed out the window. "The horde is coming back and they are going to be hungry." Hannah smiled up at him. "Welcome home, Son. We're not perfect, we make mistakes, but we're family. All of us, including you."

"Thank you." He managed to say the words, and thankfully, Hannah left him alone at the window because a man of forty-six didn't get emotional over a simple conversation.

.

CHAPTER 14

Brie opened the door to the apartment. Ryker had been a trooper, and they'd stayed until almost the last person left Amber and Brody's apartment. They'd played touch football in the vacant lot that Brody and Blay had gone in together and bought. So far, they'd fenced it in and posted it as private property for the tenants of Brody's building, but the plans they had included a playground and corner for a dog playpen where animals could play and be safe from traffic on nearby roads.

Ryker's hand found her hip. She smiled up at him. He leaned down and kissed her slowly and tenderly before he straightened. He had to be hurting and tired. She shut the door behind them and headed straight into the kitchen. "I'll get you your pills."

"Actually, I feel good." Ryker's voice floated after her.

"But you need the anti-inflammatory." She grabbed the medication bottle, read the front, put it back, and grabbed another one. *Bingo.* She opened it and shook out two. "Here you go." She held the caplets for him.

"Thank you." He took them and tossed him down his throat.

"You're supposed to take that with milk or food." She put her hands on her hips and he rolled his eyes and smiled.

"All right, I'll drink a glass of milk. Do you want anything?" He glanced back and stopped. A smile spread across his face. "I think you do."

"Oh, hell yeah." She bit her bottom lip and cocked her head. "Drink your milk, Captain, then meet me in the bedroom."

Ryker watched her hips sway as she meandered from the room after giving him a sexy smile. *Damn.* He opened the fridge, grabbed the milk, and took two huge swigs straight from the plastic jug. He recapped the moo juice, shut the fridge, and stalked through the living room toward the bedroom. He stopped at the doorway. Brie had turned down the bed and was laying in the middle of it--naked.

He shifted the strap of the sling from his neck and removed the material with a swipe of his hand. Brie walked on her knees to the end of the bed. "Let me help." Her fingertips slid under the t-shirt and traced across his abs. She unfastened his jeans and unzipped the constricting fabric. He stepped out of them and then his boxers as she peeled the material off. Carefully, she unhooked the safety pins and helped him remove the t-shirt.

He brought her to him with his good arm and found her mouth, kissing her the way he'd wanted to kiss her all afternoon. He ran his hand down her back. Her luscious curves and the soft swell of her breasts fit against him perfectly. He lifted a knee and edged her backward. She dropped as he advanced, putting her fully under him in the middle of the bed. He held his weight on his good arm and stared down at her. "How did I get so lucky?"

She reached up and pushed his hair from his face. Her eyes searched his before she smiled. "Luck has nothing to do with us. You're mine and I love you."

He lowered his lips to hers and brushed them tenderly. "You are the single best thing in my life. I never stood a chance; you stole my heart."

"And I'll never give it back." She rolled her hips under him.

He dropped his forehead to her shoulder and groaned, "Minx."

"Who, me?" She rolled her hips against his cock again and made a sound that came damn close to a purr.

She spread her legs, and he found heaven. Her fiery core gloved him in ecstasy. "God." He slid deeper and retreated, loosening her to accept him. "So fucking good." His arm supporting him trembled. He moved onto his knees, settled onto his heels, and helped her move closer to him. The injury limited the way he could pleasure her, but he'd fucking make sure she found her release. Who needed a second arm? He grabbed her hip and slowly thrust into her again. He watched a blush spread across her skin. Her breasts swayed in time with the movement of his hips. "I want to kiss you. Here." He ran his thumb across her nipple.

She panted, "Yes."

He ran his finger down her arm and cupped her hand in his, kissing the palm before he lowered it and placed it on her breast. "Show me what you'd want me to do." Her finger circled her nipple, teasing it with soft strokes.

He placed her other hand lower. "Touch yourself. Show me, baby. Show me what you like." He would not last. The woman was erotic sex personified. Her hair spread in a halo across the pillows and sheets, one hand teasing her nipple, the other... Oh hell, she spread her sex with two fingers and stroked herself. He could see his cock glistening from her excitement as he withdrew. Her fingers moved faster, and he kept pace. She arched and tightened around him, her hands slapped the sheets and fisted them seconds before her body gripped him. He let himself go and chased his own release.

It took several long seconds before he opened his eyes. The sight before him was nothing short of heaven. He carefully lowered beside her and moved her to his good side. "I don't think you'll ever understand how much I love you." He kissed the top of her head.

"I think I do. You made my life complete. It was as if I was stumbling in darkness, then finally opened my eyes and the only thing I could see, feel, or imagine was you." She wiggled closer and shrugged. "That still doesn't describe it, but..."

He trailed his good hand down her back. "No, it does, it makes perfect sense. You are my everything. I don't know what I'd do without you."

"Let's hope you never have to find out." She sighed and then yawned.

He kissed the top of her head again and listened to her breath even out as she drifted to sleep. He stared at the ceiling, terrified. Good things rarely lasted for him. Fate had a way of taking things from him. He tightened his arm around Brie. Fuck fate. He'd allow nothing to take her from him. Ever.

Ryker woke slowly. The sun had just started coming up and Brie had tangled herself around him. It had been a week since they'd shot him. Seven days with no answers and too many questions. He had to take a trip into the city today. Thankfully, he could manipulate his arm and shoulder into a button-down. He'd started physical therapy two days ago, and damn it if he didn't feel like a blubbering baby by the time the woman finished with him. Her perky attitude added insult to the injury. The *'You're doing so good'* and *'Excellent work, Captain'* were the little PT's favorite cheers, and they made him realize he'd never cared for the cheerleader type.

He stared through the window and contemplated the day. Terrence was driving him into New York. He could manage the drive, but he deferred to his doctor's orders. No driving for another two weeks. The doc had a point, not that he'd publicly admit to agreeing with him.

He and Mouse had a lot of ground to cover. She wanted to be free of Peña and Rubio, and he wanted answers. What in the hell would possess Peña to go after him? How could they prove it was in fact Peña who went after him and not one of the many people Ryker had put in jail? His team cleared that logic trail, going back through cases, checking on whereabouts of his previous collars, examining those that had been paroled and recent prison releases. As of this time, the answer was a big, fat no.

Then there was the school of thought that what had occurred was an initiation. Take out one of the big gears in HCPD to earn your way into a gang. The only problem with that line of thinking was that there had been no other attacks against officers in the HCPD, which there would have been if a gang had changed the jump-in process.

Callaway and Forsythe were still working the case, and the geofence had netted the number that called his phone right before the shooting. Unfortunately, it hadn't pinged against any tower since then. Probably resting at the bottom of a sewer drain or in the landfill without a battery. So, in the absence of any other theory, Peña took center-stage, and Mouse was the only option he had to make sense of what was going on.

His cell vibrated, but he couldn't reach it. Brie was lying on his good arm and he couldn't lift his other arm that far yet. Brie jolted awake when he moved. "It's just my phone." He watched as awareness descended on her. She sat up and carefully stretched past him, retrieving it. He used his finger to swipe the face of the phone as Brie headed, gloriously naked, into the bathroom. "Terrell."

"Hey. Do you want to meet me somewhere? I don't want to lead anyone to your new digs, just in case someone is watching." Terrence's voice was too damn chipper for this time in the morning.

"I'll go with Brie to her restaurant. Pick me up there at about..." He glanced at Brie, who was padding back to the bed. She held up her fingers, indicating ten. It would make for a late return, but it was Brie's first day back today and he wouldn't see her until after midnight. "Ten."

"Fine, but you're buying dinner." Terrence ended the call, and he dropped the phone onto his stomach. "Sorry to wake you up."

Brie made a humming noise and snuggled up next to him. "What are you doing today? The doctor said no work for two more weeks."

"I have to go into New York to talk to a witness. Someone who may have an idea why someone would go after me."

She lurched up onto her elbow, startling him. "Who is going with you?" Her eyes were a bit wild behind the fall of dark brown hair.

"Lieutenant Theron." He frowned and pushed the hair from her face with his good arm. "Don't worry, babe. I don't take unnecessary chances. What happened last week was a freak thing."

She sagged. "It was only last week, wasn't it? Sometimes it seems longer, but other times I'm right back at the hospital waiting to hear from the doctor about your injuries." She leaned her cheek into her hand. "Speaking of that, have you talked to your brothers since they stopped by the hospital that morning?"

He closed his eyes. They had all reached out to him, but he hadn't responded. He needed to return their calls and texts. "No, and that's on me. Every one of them has either called or texted. I haven't returned their gestures."

"How about we have them over for dinner on Saturday? I'm going back on a limited schedule until you go to work, and I thought I'd come home after dinner service has started. After that, it is pretty much downhill. I can do the accounting and the deposits the next day. Roger can lock up the register drawer when the front doors close." She laid down on his good shoulder and slid her long leg over his.

"Are you sure?" He turned his head so he could see her.

"Yeah, this past week I've realized just how much time I've been spending at the restaurant. I can work from ten in the morning until seven at night and handle everything. I was usually helping prep, but in reality, we can hire someone to do that. It would seem there is something in my life more important than my restaurant now. So... Saturday?"

"Saturday?" He searched his brain for any reason to postpone that event but couldn't come up with even a ghost of an excuse. "Yeah, sure. Saturday."

"Perfect. I can invite down Brody and Amber." She yawned and cuddled closer.

"No, let's hold off with that. I think the first time I meet with all of them, I should probably do it alone."

"Alone? Oh, okay, I can find something to do at the restaurant."

"No. I meant without the others. I've seen how inviting your family grows into a major affair. Just you and me this time, and we'll include the clan later. Besides, I'd like you to get to know my brothers." He ran his fingertips up and down her arm in a lazy caress.

Now that he understood what had happened on his brothers' side of their joint past, he was trying to put the pain behind him. Trying, and mostly succeeding. There were still lingering feelings that he'd have to deal with, feelings of inadequacy, of never measuring up. Benjamin had ingrained those feelings well, but perhaps that was why he'd worked so damn hard to build a successful team. Fenton reminded him of his stepfather. No matter how well he and his team worked, Fenton degraded and demoralized him. Yet he fought for his team and for himself. It was what he did, what he knew. Who knows what he would have done or become if his stepfather hadn't treated him like he was worthless?

"Dinner? I can ask Roger to make something nice and I can bring it home. That way I don't have to cook, I can visit with you and your brothers."

"That would be perfect." He chuckled when she yawned again. "Go back to sleep. We have time."

She snuggled against him and sighed. "You sure?" The words slid together. He kissed the top of her head in response. Man, what did he do to deserve a woman like her? He couldn't think of a damn thing. But that was okay. He'd take this gift and treasure her as long as God saw fit to allow him to breathe.

Brie drove into her parking slot and put her SUV into park. Her eyes went to the back door of the restaurant and a smile sprang at the sight of the camera installed above the door. She pointed to it. "Roger got it installed."

"That's good. He hasn't told you of anything else happening out here, right?" Ryker unfastened his seatbelt as he spoke.

She opened her door to avoid looking at him. "He hasn't said a word." Which wasn't a lie. She'd never told him about what happened to her, but she knew Roger would call her if those two assholes were intimidating anyone else. Since talking to Bekki, the dots connecting the two assholes and Councilman Davis seemed to make sense. Bullying and intimidation for graft or kickbacks. How many businesses were paying the man just to exist?

A silver SUV entered the alleyway. Ryker exited the truck, and after they both shut the doors, she locked the vehicle. "That's my ride." He tugged her in and dropped a sweet kiss on her lips. "I look forward to spending more nights together. But remember, if you need to be here, I understand."

"See, the thing is, I really don't. They are doing just fine without me. If I change my hours, they'll continue to do well. But tonight, I may be late. I have a weeks' worth of paperwork to get through." She rose on her toes and kissed him again. The SUV coasted to a stop beside them and Lieutenant

Theron rolled down the window. "Ready to go? Hey, Brie, how are you?"

"I'm good. Take care of him for me?" She chuckled at the bear-like growl Ryker made at that comment.

"No worries. I'll keep him out of trouble." Terrence laughed at the middle finger Ryker presented him.

"I'll see you at the apartment later." He kissed her one last time. A dark green late model car drove up behind the SUV and honked politely. Ryker glanced at the car and then back at her. "I love you."

"Love you, too. Get going before you cause a traffic jam." She watched him get into the SUV and waved as they departed. The middle-aged couple in the car waiting behind the SUV waved to her as they followed the SUV from the alley.

She jogged to the stairs and entered the morning chaos of a kitchen prepping for service. Someone shouted a greeting and then welcomes and questions swamped her. The sense of belonging and of community wrapped around her like a comfortable sweater that warmed her down to her soul.

She stopped by the station where her chef was

working. "Roger, when you get to a point you can take a break, come in so we can talk?"

He glanced up for a minute from the vat of bolognaise he was stirring. "Sure. The receipts are on your desk, separated by day. Last night's drawer is in the safe. There are a couple issues we need to talk about, but I've managed workarounds for them until you can devise something better. We're booked for three weeks solid for dinner service and we've sold out of specials five out of the six days for lunch service." He grabbed a spoon from one of the many containers near his station and tasted his creation. "Needs more garlic and salt. Give me some time to make this right and I'll pop in. Your office is open and your keys are on your desk."

"Perfect. Thank you." She opened the door to her closet-sized office and drew a deep breath. Stacks of paperwork neatly arranged with stickies on the top of each showing the day the papers arrived sat waiting for her. She draped her purse handle on the back of her chair and sat down. Time to make up for the week she'd taken off. The paperwork version of penance.

She blinked and looked up at the knock on her door. "You ready?" Roger stood in her doorway. He was wiping his hands on the towel that hung from his apron.

"Sure. Everything here is self-explanatory except for the receipts from vendors we haven't used before. I'm assuming we are still having problems with our primary vendors?" *Three vendors, to be exact.*

"Yeah. It isn't ringing true in my books. I talked with other chefs. Those businesses are delivering to them." Roger sat down in the chair across from her desk. "What's the real story here?"

She leaned forward. "I'm not sure, but what I'm going to tell you goes no further than that doorway. You can't say anything, understand?"

"Sure, you know you can trust me, Boss." Roger leaned forward, lessening the space between them.

"I think I'm being squeezed in order to get my initiative through the city's red tape and for approval."

Roger's face turned a dark red. "That is absolute bullshit, Brie." He shook his head. "You're trying to help those less fortunate and someone is squeezing you? Who is it?"

"I don't know." She had major suspicions, but Roger didn't need to have that information. "I've asked my sister Bekki to look into what is going on. I'm going to give her the name of the vendors that have suddenly been unable to fulfill our orders and let her go to work. Anything we say about this could derail her investigation, so we are going to be mute on this problem. Got it?"

"Yeah. I don't like it, but I get it." He glanced at the door before he stood and started back toward the kitchen. "My pasta is ready. I need to sheet it and start the raviolis."

"I'll finish with this and call Bekki. I need to talk with you and Lola after lunch service."

Roger stopped, spun, and asked, "Something wrong?"

"No. Not at all. Just a couple changes I want to make. Oh, and thank you for installing the camera."

"It was really easy. The battery will last a month, so I set up a recurring reminder on your computer to remind you when to pull it and charge it. There is a folder on the system's desktop where the videos are accessible. I set it to keep them for a week, then delete them. The owner's manual is in your top desk drawer." He shouted the last words as he walked back into the kitchen.

Ryker's injury had changed her in so many ways, and yet her world was just the same as it was when she stepped away a week ago. The familiar chatter, occasional shouted orders, and laughter faded into the background. *Where it should be*, a small voice inside her head reminded her. She'd built a successful business and had a great team in place. Working normal hours while still providing the leadership necessary wasn't impossible. She'd just need to tweak her schedule if problems came up, and those nights that Ryker would be busy she would stay at work and help. It was… *liberating and scary*. She'd worked so hard for so long, taking a step back seemed like a luxury, although it wasn't —it was just the reward for all the hard work she'd invested into her pride and joy.

She shook her head, clearing away the meandering thoughts, and grabbed her cell. Scrolling down to her sister's number, she called Bekki.

"What's up?" Her sister seemed distracted.

"Is this a bad time?" Her information could wait. Bekki worked on several stories at a time.

"Huh? No, no. I'm just frustrated. What's on your mind?"

"Well, remember I told you about the vendors that weren't filling our orders anymore?"

"Like it was yesterday."

"Well, there are three, and they have consistently declined to fill our orders while filling other restaurants, at least according to my chef."

"Okay. Could you do me a favor? I'm not in the office. Could you text me the names of the vendors and the dates of your orders? Hell, even a copy of your orders would help." Bekki sounded like she was walking in a crowded building.

"I can scan them and send you an email."

"That would be perfect. Hey, have you heard from Blay lately?"

She frowned as she thought. "No. I haven't seen him since Sunday dinner at Brody's. Why?"

"Nothing. I need help to navigate some construction permits and since he's Builder Bob, I thought he could point me in the right direction. I don't want to bother Brody at work."

"But you'll bother Blay?"

"Ha, well, yeah. Unless he's putting out a fire, he's just lazing around, right?" Bekki laughed loudly.

"You know, I don't think that's how it is at the firehouse." She knew Blay worked hard. What he did all day if there wasn't a call she wasn't sure, but she couldn't picture Blay with his feet kicked up watching television along with the rest of the station.

"Whatever. He needs to call me back." Bekki snorted the reply.

"And when did you call him?"

"About… ten minutes ago."

She snorted at Bekki's impatience. "Give him a half-hour before you call him again. He might be doing something important."

"Again, whatever. Doesn't he know that his world rotates around me?" Bekki cackled an evil laugh.

"You're horrible."

"Nah, I'm perfect. Look, I got to go. My Uber is pulling up. Send me that email and I'll look into it. Don't engage with these guys, just find a work-around until I get answers."

"We've done that." Or rather, Roger had done that.

"Okay. I'll call as soon as I have anything. Got to fly. Bye." The line went dead.

She shifted the phone away from her ear. "Bye." Her sister personified perpetual energy that seemed wound just a bit too tight. She was a wonderful person but a lot to take if you didn't know her. Well, even if you knew her, she was a lot to handle. With a chuckle, she grabbed the orders that her vendors didn't fill and scanned them into the computer. She needed to get through the paperwork so she could meet Ryker at home tonight. A smile filled her heart. She had a reason to leave work. Damn, could life get any better?

CHAPTER 15

R yker sat down in the rehab facility's intake room. The need to speak with Mouse privately put them in the small room. He looked up when the door opened.

"What happened to you?" Mouse froze just inside the door. She looked better. Her skin held a pink tint instead of the grey pallor she'd had the last time they'd met. Her hair was clean and secured in a ponytail, her eyes were clear, but there were still dark rings under them.

"A bullet." He would not pull any punches with her.

"Because of me?" She leaned against the wall instead of sitting down across from him.

"I think so. Care to fill me in?"

She looked down at her fingers she'd knotted in the hem of her hospital scrub top. "They couldn't have found you through me. I was careful."

"You used your friend Alice to reach out to me. They found Alice floating. They knew my number. Anyone with any connections can find the name to go with a telephone number. Peña and Rubio have many, many connections." He shifted in the chair so he was facing her.

Tears welled in her eyes and then traveled down her cheeks. "Alice didn't deserve that. She only sent a text."

"Why are they after you, Mouse?"

"Don't call me that." Mouse snapped before she sniffed and wiped her nose on the long T-shirt she wore under her scrubs. "My name is Sarah."

He nodded. "Why are they after you, Sarah?"

"They paid off Dexter. They own me." She shrugged.

"Dexter was your pimp?" He clicked his pen and started writing before he pushed the chair across from him with his foot and nodded to it.

Sarah moved across the room and sat down. "Pimp, drug supplier. Yeah. I didn't lie to you. Peña and Rubio bought four of us for that party. That was sometime last summer." She sobbed and closed her eyes. "I was the lucky one. They chose me to stay. The others... Peña gave Lacey to his guards. I could hear her screaming and crying. That went on for days and then... it didn't."

"They kill her?" Ryker stared at his informant.

She nodded. "They carried her out. She was dead. OD or they did it. I don't know which."

"The others?" He waited for an answer.

"I don't know. Didn't see them after that." Sarah wiped her nose with her sleeve again.

"Tell me what happened to you." He leaned back in his chair.

"When you get picked, you get new clothes. They give you prime drugs. But man, the shit I did. I let them fuck me whenever they wanted. Rubio is into that sadistic shit. He liked it when I cried and begged, but only when he said I could. Peña liked to watch, or he liked to fuck me at the same time Rubio did." She sniffed again. "Peña and Rubio are together."

"You mean like a couple?" Ryker leaned forward.

"Yeah. I was wasted most of the time, but they were lovers. They only fucked me when Rubio wanted to get his freak on or when others were around. It was a secret. I was their cover." She shoved her finger in her mouth and started chewing on her nail. "I knew I had to get out of there. I started acting like I was high, but I did less and less. Man, I fucking wanted it. Needed it, but I knew that one day I was going to take flight and not land, you know? They were getting careless around me. Talking business. Naming names. There was another party scheduled. They were talking about buying some new girls. They were going to kill me. They didn't say it, but I knew." She shrugged. "I waited until they started fucking. The guards didn't pay me any mind anymore. I floated around like I was high and went into the bathroom. I opened the window, slid down the outside of the house and I ran. I hid at the Cottages, but they went there looking for me. I found Alice. I knew her from before. She was still with Dexter."

"What names did you hear? I'll need everything, Sarah. Everything."

"Did they shoot you?"

"Yeah, we think so."

"Because I reached out to you?" She stared at him, and the desolation in her eyes begged him to say no. He nodded, and she closed her eyes. "I'm fucking poison."

"No, you are the person who is going to stop these two men from hurting more people. You are the only person who can do it. Work with me, Sarah, and help me take down this organization." Ryker leaned forward and placed his hand on her arm. "You deserve justice for what they did to you, and to Lacey, and to Alice, and so many more. Help us take them down."

Sarah opened her eyes. "What if what I have isn't enough?"

"It's enough, and on the off chance it isn't, it will start the ball rolling. You're listed as a CI. Mouse is the only name in my documentation. No one is going to know your actual name, and when they learn it in court, it will be too late because we can get you into the Witness Protection Program and no one will ever find you. No one is going to know where you are going. You can make a difference and then live a life outside what these fuckers did to you. No one needs to know. You can go back to school and become whatever you want to be."

"It can't be that simple." Her words were a thin whisper.

"Oh, I didn't say it was going to be simple. You need to kick the drug demon riding you. That won't be easy, and you'll have to deal with that every day. You need to make an investment in yourself. No, life isn't easy Sarah, but it can be so damn good."

"Yeah?" She looked up at him, desperate to cling to any hope.

"Yeah. That I promise."

"Okay. What do you want to know?"

"First off, I want to bring in my lieutenant so he can write while we talk. I don't want any distractions when we talk. Also, can I record our conversation?"

Sarah glanced at his phone and then at the door. "Yeah, okay."

Ryker stood and went to the door opposite of where Mouse had walked in and called in Terrence. "Sarah, you remember Lieutenant Terrence Theron." He put his phone on the charging cord and plugged it in, starting the voice recording app. He introduced himself and Terrence again and asked Sarah on the recording if he could record the conversation. She agreed, and they began.

Eight hours later, Ryker and Terrence shut themselves into Terrence's SUV. "Holy fuck, Ry.

She gave us everything we need to take down both of those bastards."

"Several of his key people, too. Hell, she listed names we'd never suspected and tied them to the operation." Ryker turned and looked at his lieutenant. "I'll call the Deputy Commissioner. Based on Sarah's information, we can get a search warrant for Pena's hit squad's location, the warehouse, and the cash counting operation."

"That's why they went after you. They'd fucked up and let Mouse slip through their fingers. They'd scheduled her replacement. Who knows how long she would have lasted if she hadn't run?" Terrence put the truck into reverse and pulled from the parking space.

He nodded and called up the Deputy Commissioner's home telephone number. It was dark already. He'd call Brie after he reported in. He glanced at his watch. After a week gone, he'd probably beat her home even with the three-hour drive and countless telephone calls he'd need to make to arrange his team's responses. Check that. With the information he had, they might have warrants issued by the time they got back. It would be at least twenty-four hours before he'd be able to pull away from the operation. Hell, if push came to shove, he'd sleep at the team building in one of the holding cells. They'd all done that before at one time or another. He'd be lucky to see her in a week. But she knew what life with a cop was like. Damn, he was fucking lucky to have the woman he loved and a job that mattered. He nodded to himself as he called his new boss. He wasn't lying when he told Sarah life could be damn good.

Brie stretched her back and glanced at the clock. Her conversation with Lola and Roger hadn't gone as expected. It had gone better.

"It's about time, Brie. You can't keep living at this place." Lola smiled. *"Oh, can I make a suggestion?"*

She blinked back her surprise. "Sure."

"Let's get an assistant hostess to work the lunch crowd and the start of the dinner service. I'll take over from her and deal with the receipts like I did last week. I'll put the cash drawer into the safe after service and Roger can give me any information he has on vendors and deliveries. You can come in the next morning and work until I get here, and we can do a changeover."

She narrowed her eyes at both of them. "You've been giving this some thought, haven't you?"

Roger smiled. "Yeah, we've been talking. And that idea about another restaurant, I've put that on hold. I don't see Matthew much as it is. If it is all right with you, we'll just start using more of the product I want to use."

"All right, that's fine with me. I didn't want to let either of you down."

Roger chuckled. "Yeah, that's why we figured this out. Your heart is so big that if we didn't have a plan or said one negative word, you would have shelved the idea to have a life for yourself, wouldn't you?"

She considered his question for a moment. "Probably."

Brie chuckled to herself and glanced at her watch. It was only seven. She stood up and grabbed her purse. She would get home first and make dinner. Okay, well, she'd take some of Roger's bolognese sauce and make some pasta and a salad. They could have a glass of wine and watch the boats in the harbor.

After locking her office door, she wandered through the busy dinner service, snagging the quart of the bolognese sauce she'd asked Roger to hold for her from the walk-in fridge. She made sure Lola saw her and waved at both her and Roger before she headed to the back door.

She stood on the top steps and drew a deep breath of the cool air. The alley light was broken again, but the light above the door to the restaurant cast a glow for quite a distance. She stared at the parking spots and chided herself for worrying. Glancing up at the small camera above the door, she mentally thanked Roger once again for installing the equipment. Regardless, she put her hand in her purse and wrapped her finger around the butt of her gun. Her finger was not on the trigger, but she was ready to defend herself should she need to do so. Her mom and dad didn't raise a fool.

The crunch of rocks under her shoes made her jump. Damn, she was wound tight. There was nothing and no one around. She laughed at herself and let go of the gun, fishing for her keys.

"Welcome back, bitch."

Brie spun, grabbing for the gun in her purse. She knew that voice. Blondie. *Fuck, fuck, fuck!*

"It would seem you are in the wrong place at the wrong time, my friend." Another voice spun her again. A man with slicked back black hair and a diamond earring the size of her fist stared at Blondie but moved his arm suddenly. She gasped and pushed herself back into the truck. The end of a nasty-looking suppressor was pointed directly at her.

"Who the fuck are you?" the blond man snarled. He held a gun, one he hadn't had before. Blondie lifted it and pointed it at the man who held a gun on her.

"None of your business." A third man said from the darkness beyond the one who was pointing a gun toward her. Two muffled pops knocked Blondie into the wall. He seemed to lose the ability to stand and slowly slid down the brick wall while staring in the direction of the man who shot him. Blondie tried to lift the gun again, and the shadow man who shot him moved forward and put a bullet between Blondie's eyes.

She gasped, but the muzzle of that suppressor pushed against her head.

"Shut up." The snarled command from Earring Dude registered when almost nothing else was making sense. Fear gripped her in its claws, and she froze. Froze. She didn't move, couldn't move. Her gun was in her purse. All she had to do was move her hand.

A scraping noise and then rapid footsteps sounded in the darkness. The second man bolted down the darkened alley. The first man gripped her bicep in a crushing hold. She heard a strangled cry and then a startled plea before those horrendous pops punctuated the alley. Three. One after the other. She slid her hand in her purse and found her gun and thumbed the safety. "Why are you doing this?"

"Shut up!" The man holding her jerked her toward him and shook her so hard her head snapped back painfully. There was no decision. No debate, and no doubt when he yanked her in close. She acted.

Brie pulled the trigger.

Twice.

She didn't hear her weapon fire, but she felt the buck of the gun in her hand. Her arm freed instantly, and she stumbled but scrambled from the man at her feet and ran. She sprinted toward the back door of the restaurant, to people and to safety. She heard the steps behind her and felt a massive weight force her forward and off-balance. Her hand flew from her purse and the entire thing went flying as she tried to stop her crash to the asphalt. She braced for it. The pavement jarred her knees. She twisted to avoid hitting her head, but it was hopeless. A smack of stabbing pain plummeted her into oblivion.

CHAPTER 16

B rie regained consciousness in stages. The pain registered first. Her face hurt like a bitch and her neck was so damn sore. She tried to lift her hand to her head. A tug brought her fully awake. Someone had tied her hands together with wide leather cuffs and attached the cuffs to a bar that spread her legs at her ankles. She laid on her side on a carpeted floor.

They had shoved a hard ball of some sort between her teeth. The wide stretch of her jaw hurt, or perhaps it was the way the strap pulled tight, keeping the ball in her mouth. She blinked to clear her vision. There was a sliver of light creeping under the door across from her. She heard a door slam and yelling. What language was that? She strained to hear more. The voices were indistinct, but one thing was clear—the man doing most of the yelling was mad. She panted through the feeling of nausea and tried desperately to remember…

She groaned and closed her eyes. She'd shot someone. Oh, God. Had she killed him? Tears formed and creeped over her nose, dripping to the carpet. Laying on her side, she couldn't wipe them away, but it didn't matter. The people who'd killed those two men in the alley had her. She closed her eyes and tried to calm down. When Ryker discovered she wasn't home, he'd come looking for her. Wait. Roger! Roger would see her truck was still there. He'd see the dead bodies, he'd sound the alarm, but when? What time was it now? How long before she could expect help, and would anyone know where to find her? The tears rolled faster.

A streak of clarity split her terror-filled thoughts. She'd witnessed that man kill Blondie and heard him kill the other man. She'd seen his face. Reality clipped her on the chin with the power of a right hook.

She wasn't getting out of this.

The men's voices got louder. The light under the door modulated as the men, now directly outside the door, argued. The door slammed open. The sudden light blinded her. She blinked wildly to regain her vision. The two men shouted at each other and gestured to her. They switched to English when the tall one noticed she was conscious.

"Fucking bitch." He yelled at her, spittle flying from his mouth as he raged. "You're very lucky you didn't kill him, otherwise I'd flay the skin off you, inch by inch."

Oh, God. The man she'd shot. She tried to push away from the man as he advanced. "We are going to find her, and when we do, we are going to kill you both!"

Another man jogged to them. "The doctor, he's here." The man screaming at her turned and ran from the room. The one who remained stared at her and then went back to the door and shut it but turned on the light in the room.

A bed, dresser, and nightstands were the reason for the shadows she'd seen before they turned the light on. He sat down on the end of the bed and dropped his elbows to his knees, still staring at her. His sculptured features were a bit too narrow to be handsome, but he wasn't what she expected. His clothes were nice. He wore slacks, leather slip-on shoes, was cleanly shaved, and his hair was swept back from his forehead, held with gel. She spent as much time examining him as he did her. Finally, he spoke. "It seems I am now in the center of a very messy situation. The men who have taken you have made critical errors. I don't plan on paying the price these errors will cost. You are my ticket away from their impending demise." He chuckled when her eyebrows drew tight in confusion. "A simple snatch-and-grab. Stupid. They've been doing too much of their product. They had it in their mind that they could get Terrell to give up that whore by holding you for ransom. You blew that out of the water when you shot Peña. I can't blame you, but I wish you had better aim. Now I must kill both of them. That will be... difficult as they have loyal followers. Your captain will have a choice to make. I wonder what he'll do."

Brie shook her head. She knew whatever they were trying to pressure Ryker into was horrendous and Ryker would break the law he'd spent his life upholding. Besides, she'd witnessed them kill one man, and probably another. Tears dripped off the bridge of her nose. Those men had wanted to use her to make Ryker break the law. He'd face an impossible decision. She closed her eyes and shook her head again. He wouldn't—no, couldn't—give in to criminals.

"Yes, that is exactly what I thought, too." He stood and put his hands on his hips. "Sometimes people lose touch of the ideal of a business for profit versus a lifestyle. *'Absolute power corrupts absolutely.'* I believe that is the saying used by many. It is true. Unfortunately for you, they forgot that the business can sustain loss and still be profitable."

He turned to walk away, and Brie screamed behind the gag, begging him to let her go. He stopped and stood there, facing the door for a moment. "They declared war when they tried to kill your police captain. Now... well, the business will suffer from their delusions of grandeur. I need a few hours to arrange things, then I'll be back for you. Hopefully, during my absence, Peña doesn't die and Rubio doesn't kill you."

Ryker leaned back and looked down the table at his team. In anticipation of the warrants coming through, Deputy Commissioner Duckworth had formed an interdepartmental strike force led by

Ryker's JDET team. There were three buildings they'd descend upon simultaneously. Right now, only his sergeant, lieutenant, and Tiernan Conner, the captain in charge of the SWAT teams they'd use, were present. The Deputy Commissioner was to his right.

"Do you have everything you need?" Deputy Commissioner Duckworth picked up the stack of paperwork she'd been working through.

"Yes ma'am, I believe we do." He glanced at Tiernan. "You good?"

"We are," Tiernan nodded. "As soon as we get these blueprints uploaded to the computer systems, my men and I will develop a plan of attack. We'll be ready."

"I'll brief Commissioner King. I believe someone in this room is still on medical leave." She turned her dark brown eyes on him and pegged him with a stare.

"I am. I promise I won't lift anything bigger than my cell phone."

Fuck. Speaking of cell phones, he hadn't called Brie. From the moment he'd placed the first call until this moment, he'd focused on nothing but the case. He glanced at the clock. Damn, it was almost eleven. He'd call her when the meeting broke up.

She'd probably still be working at the restaurant, especially after a week away.

"See that you don't. I won't keep you away from this, but you are in the command vehicle. I find out you violate that order and I'll bust your ass to beat cop and put you in the Desert. Copy?" Deputy Commissioner Duckworth was a ball buster and a damn good cop.

He tried not to smile, but he'd started his career in the Desert as a beat cop. Going back there wouldn't be a hardship, although at almost forty-seven, working patrol again would be a grind. "Yes ma'am. I copy."

She nodded and glanced at the rest of the men in the room. "Gentlemen, get your people organized. You've got seven hours until we pop those doors and hopefully take down Peña and Rubio once and for all."

He waited until she left and asked for the blueprints. Once they had them unrolled and weighted down with coffee cups and soda cans so they wouldn't curl in on themselves he spoke to his team leads. "Three locations at one time. It's not the biggest sweep we've ever done, but the locations bridge a wide area. Team commanders will have comms on a common frequency so the command vehicle can keep you apprised. That's you, you, and you—" he pointed at Tiernan, Brody, and Terrence, "and I want Patel, Driggers, and Montoya in the command vehicle. Those three have the most experience with command and control in these types of scenarios."

"You got it." Brody scribbled a note to himself.

Ryker stared at the maps. "According to Sarah, Peña and Rubio go nowhere without each other."

She'd given them three locations where they would be hiding. "According to her, Location One is where they've drywalled bales of money in the walls. Terrence, I want you there. Seizures of assets of this magnitude will require us to be anal with the paperwork and chain of custody. Make sure you take Mozinga, Turner, and Hayes. They can set up a count station while you and the rest of the team close all avenues of ingress or egress. Document everything with video. Once SWAT has cleared the building and you take control, nobody, and I mean nobody, goes in without my express authorization. The money haul will bring the entire alphabet soup to the table, but they don't get to look for serial numbers until we have all the evidence cataloged."

"We'll be thorough." Terrence tapped the blueprints. "I'll pull tripods and cameras from the equipment room and we'll float the video to the cloud and maintain a digital file."

"Excellent. Brody, I want you on Location Number Three. According to Mouse, that's where Peña's death squads crash. We want to surprise them." He glanced up at Tiernan. "I need massive confusion inside that house. I don't want any casualties on either side. If we can flip even *one* of those fuckers, we'll have closure on a litany of cases."

Tiernan nodded. "We've got spotlights, speakers, flashbangs, and speed on our side. My guys will wear ear and eye protection, and we've practiced with these weapons of mass confusion. They are the best bet to get in and take charge of a volatile situation like this."

"Good." Ryker leveled his stare on his sergeant. "You let SWAT clear the house, then separate, process, and transport those men here. If we have too many for our holding cells, I want one of ours wherever we put these guys on ice. I don't want them talking to anyone but us or their lawyers. Copy?"

Brody nodded. "We'll have a patrol sit on them if they need ambulance transport to a hospital."

"Good call. We have the Deputy Commissioner's permission to use precinct-specific assets if needed. I'll make sure the command vehicle officers have that information. Call it in if needed and we'll get dispatch to send in what backup you need." Ryker turned to Tiernan. "Location Two is where we believe Peña and Rubio are going to be. The warehouse had seven points of egress. My people can secure the outside until your people clear the building. According to Mouse, they converted the upper level into a living area. Downstairs is where they keep the drugs. Get this, the drugs are in semi-trailers. They back in, unhook the drug trailer, hook up to an empty, and head back to fill up again."

"Fucking industrious of them, isn't it?" Tiernan snipped. "I'll call in another team. The square footage of this building requires it. If your people can cover the exits, we'll sweep through the bottom as soundlessly as we can and work our way up. The structure prevents a rooftop down approach, and unlike the guys on television, we're not going to rappel from the roof into a hostile environment. I kinda like my guys, plan on keeping them alive."

"Not getting dead is our goal every day." He sent a sweeping look at the three men with him.

"Peña and Rubio are rattlesnakes, but they like the comfort and the sense of invincibility their money buys. We are striking a major blow in the morning. Let's get our shit together and get ready."

Brody handed him the blueprints. "SWAT has their copies, these are your copies for the command truck."

"Thank you. What team is Amber on?"

"She's with Rayburn and Watson on team one."

Brody walked with him toward his office. "I can't believe they've put money into the walls of the houses and drywalled over them. What if it fucking burns down? Idiots."

Ryker chuckled and nodded toward his office. "I'm sure it sounded like a good idea at the time. Get your shit together, you don't need to babysit me."

"Now, Cap, would I do that?" Brody laughed when Ryker flipped him off as he retrieved his cell phone from his pocket. "Now that I'm living with your sister, yeah, you would."

Brody shrugged and raised a hand as he went to Theron's office, no doubt to split up the thirty officers assigned to JDET.

Ryker opened his phone, scrolled to Brie's number, and called. It rang through to voicemail. He glanced at the clock. Unusual. He dropped the blueprints onto his desk and sat down, taking his arm from the sling. He pushed her number again, and the phone went to voice-mail again. A tremble of unease rolled across him.

The phone rang and he jumped to answer it, but the call wasn't from Brianna, it was from her brother, Brock.

He slid his thumb across the face and barked, "What happened?"

"Is Brie with you?"

"No. I'm at work. Where are you?"

"Horizon. We have a double homicide and a pool of blood we can't identify. Brie's purse was on the ground by the back door, mixed with what we determined was a broken bottle of sauce. We've looked everywhere, but we can't find her phone."

"Did anyone see what happened?"

"The chef is pulling the tapes from the new camera system. He said Brie left about seven-thirty. Hang on, he's got it up."

"Fuck, I'm on my way." He darted from his office and headed to the pegboard that held the vehicles assigned to the precinct.

"Ryker, have you tried to call her?"

He closed his eyes for a second. "It went to

voicemail. Twice."

"Okay, I'm putting you on mute while I watch the video, standby."

Brock went silent as Brody and Terrence jogged toward him. "What's up?" Brody asked as they approached.

He held the phone away from his face as he filled in Brody. "Double homicide outside of Horizon. Brie's missing."

"Missing? Fuck, I'll drive." Brody fished his keys from his pocket.

"Terrence, call the Deputy Commissioner and let her know what is happening. Pull in Thompson and Dodson, bring them up to speed just in case we don't get back in time." He headed to the door with Brody in tow as he shouted his commands.

"How long has she been missing?" Brody asked.

"Hold on," he answered as they got into Brody's truck. "Come on, Brock, tell me what's on that video."

"We have it. The clip is grainy, and it's dark. It looks like she may have injured one of the men that trapped her. We have Subject One on tape shooting Subject Two and then running into the darkness in the direction we found the other body, Subject Three. Something happened and Brie got loose. The shooter, Subject One, tackled her. Her head bounced hard on the asphalt. He drove up in a late model blue SUV with chrome bumpers. No plate. He threw her in the back and loaded the man she evidently injured and escaped from, Subject Four, into the front. By the amount of blood where he fell, she had to have shot him or maybe stabbed him, trying to get away. I know she has a concealed carry permit. Was she packing heat? Did something happen?"

"She had her tire slashed a while back. That's why she had the video camera installed." Brody hit the lights and siren and took the corner out of the parking lot on two wheels. Ryker grabbed the 'Oh, shit' bar with his good arm and pinned his phone to his ear with his weak arm. "Can you get an ID on the video?"

"We've already sent it to tech, but the original is still on her computer. If this is related to the attack on you, my bet is you can ID the guys." Brock sighed. "I've seen some half-faced surveillance photos of Rubio and Peña. These guys could be them. Same size, but I don't know."

"Fuck. All right. Have you called your father?"

"No. I haven't. I don't want to make that call." Brock's voice shook. "They are letting me stay, but for obvious reasons, it isn't my case. Get here before they pull me away. I'll call Dad." Brock ended the call.

"What did he say?" Brody swerved around one of the few vehicles on the road that didn't bother to get the hell out of his way.

Ryker explained what Brock had relayed. "She's not dead." Brody spoke the words, probably to reassure himself.

Ryker nodded in agreement and ground his teeth together. If she'd killed one of those bastards, the other would make her pay, and from the horror stories that Mouse had told him, he prayed for that bastard to live.

They slid to a stop at the entrance to the alleyway and both of them sprinted under the yellow crime scene tape. Brody flashed his badge, stopping the uniforms on the perimeter from giving chase. They followed the cleared area to the back door of the restaurant.

Ryker tried to breathe on the way to Brie's office. It wasn't working. An iron fist squeezed his chest with relentless pressure. Brock stood beside another detective. "Play it again." Ryker tried again to control his breathing as he focused on the screen.

"Motherfucker. That's Peña," Brody said, his chest heaving just like Ryker's.

Ryker pointed to the second man who moved forward.

"Yes, that's Peña. This man is Rubio. I don't have a clue who the blond man is." The video showed Rubio put a bullet in the man's brain. "Was."

Ryker watched as Rubio bolted down the alley and Brie struggled with Peña. There was no way to tell what happened, but Peña went down and Brie flew toward the back door of the restaurant. That's when Rubio tackled her. Both he and Brody winced at the violent way her head hit the pavement. *Fuck.*

"Dad's on his way," Brock said as the video stopped.

Ryker's phone vibrated, and he glanced down at it. An unknown number. "Unknown number. Keep quiet." Everyone in the room stopped and waited.

He swiped the face. "Captain Ryker Terrell."

"She is alive."

"Who is this and how can I know for sure you're not lying?" People were scrambling quietly to put a trace on his telephone number.

The cool, cultured voice with only the slightest

trace of an accent said, "I am a businessman who has a vested interest in your woman staying alive."

"Businessman. You mean competitor." Ryker glanced at Brody who gave him a hand signal telling him they'd started a trace on his number.

"I wasn't until tonight."

"Ah, then someone who is rising from among the ranks."

"Someone that knows business doesn't benefit from a war with the police department."

"You think if you give her back unharmed that I won't pursue you?"

There was a laugh at the other end of the line. "I would be deeply disappointed if you did not chase. That *is* the game, after all. Now, I must go liberate your woman. Be at the Pier Point dock in forty-five minutes. Come alone or she dies. I don't want a war, Captain, but I will fight one if need be."

Ryker swore when he realized the man had disconnected. *It hadn't been long enough for a trace, had it?*

Brody listened on his phone and closed his eyes. He shook his head as he disconnected the call.

"Damn it."

"You can't go." The detective that Brock was standing by spoke for the first time since they'd entered the office.

"The hell I can't." Ryker pushed his way from the office.

The cop grabbed his good arm. "He'll kill both of you."

"He may." Ryker jerked his arm from the man's grasp. "Brody, Brock, with me."

"You can't go. This is my investigation." The man damn near screamed the command.

Ryker spun on the man and let the rage he felt loose. "No! The double homicide outside was your investigation. It is tied to a JDET case. You have zero authority over a damn thing involving it, so stand the fuck down before I put you on your ass!"

"Captain Terrell!"

He spun at his name, barely controlling the rage seething through him. Commissioner King strode through the front of the restaurant. "Brody, Brock, you and the Captain meet me in the front."

"But–" Ryker motioned to his phone.

"I know you're not questioning my order, are you, Captain?"

"No, sir." He fumed and marched to the front of the restaurant. He could hear Chauncey talking, but he didn't give a fuck. He was going in after Brie and nothing was going to stop him. He flung the door open and stopped dead. Two SWAT vehicles were idling on the curb. Colonel Hodgkins, the man in charge of the Special Weapons and Tactics branch of HCPD, motioned to the command vehicle. "We need to know what you have."

He glanced at Brody and then Brock. They all turned when Brie's father slammed the front door of the restaurant open. "We're wasting time." He marched past them. "What do you have?"

Ryker followed him. "Rubio took her. We believe she critically injured Peña because of the blood evidence left. But... I received a call about five minutes ago." He relayed the conversation word for word.

Chauncey smoothed his mustache. "Walt, we need that area covered. Soundlessly. If that bastard sees anything, he'll kill my girl. Ryker, you aren't going in light. We need body armor and I want him wired, and he needs to hear us without this fucker seeing an earpiece. Can you provide that?"

"We can. I'll have it brought to the rally point."

"No. No rally point. If this guy is really from Peña's crew, he'll have eyes on the street. We need to slip in." Ryker stopped the conversation. "We know Peña's crew. They are going to follow the money. Sure, there will be a few faithful to Rubio and Peña, but that's his problem if he's going to force a coup."

"Will he be able to organize so quickly?" the Colonel asked.

"He'll have a backbone in place. He'd be a fool to take on those two without some support."

"Then we move in silently. Let the men take their personal vehicles to darkened parking areas close enough to get us there and set up. We need to move now." The Colonel looked at Chauncey. He glanced at Ryker. "Will it work?"

"Our best shot is me going in alone. If you're not allowing that, then yes, silent from numerous points, and not one team moving from a single point would cause less suspicion."

"Do it." The Commissioner's words caused a chain reaction of movement. He glanced at Ryker. "You've got to keep your head about you. You will be the difference between Brie coming away from this alive or not."

"Sir, I'm the reason they brought Brie into this."

"Bullshit." Chauncey held up a hand. "The blame for this is firmly on Peña and Rubio."

Brock cleared his throat. "Do you really think this new player will take out the top of the organization?"

Ryker shrugged. "At this point, I'm praying he does. He doesn't want a war, and that's what he'd get if something happens to Brie."

Brody scratched his cheek. "I don't know if he knows who she is. Do you think any of them did the research other than perhaps seeing you two together someplace?"

Ryker nodded. "There was a car in the alley. A middle-age couple. I didn't give that vehicle a second thought. Damn it."

"Why would you?" The Commissioner moved to take the body armor that the Colonel handed him.

"This is the latest body armor we have. Here is the earpiece. The mic attaches to the body armor and we double-checked the battery."

"Do you have a weapon?" Chauncey tugged the loop-and-hook tape, opening the armor.

Ryker lifted his leg and removed his off-duty weapon from his ankle holster. The small nine-millimeter would not take down a tank, but it would stop someone if he was close enough.

"That will work. We'll figure a way to lodge it

in a sling, but we'll need a cloth one, not these straps."

"Here." Brody peeled off his light blue long sleeve shirt, leaving him wearing a black t-shirt. "Tie the arms together. The material is dense enough they won't be able to see the gun."

"He'll suspect something." Brock helped Ryker take off the other sling.

"Yeah, that's the idea." Brie's father tied a knot in the sleeve, and they worked together to get his arm back into the triangle of material. "If he is focusing on Ryker, it will give us more opportunity to get our people into position."

"Do a radio check and then get yourself to the pier at the right time." Chauncey stopped and leveled a stare at Ryker. "I know you love her, Son, but being a hero and dying will not do her any good. I want you both out of this alive and well. Understand?"

Ryker gulped past the lump in his throat. He nodded rather than spoke. Words right now were beyond him. People caring when the chips were down.

This was family.

His family.

CHAPTER 17

B rie snapped her eyes open. The thunderous sounds of many heavy footsteps moved past the room they held her in. She closed her eyes again and listened closely. There was a knock on a door down the hall. A few words and a startled yell. Gunfire popped with horrendous clarity. At least ten or fifteen shots. Shouted words echoed loudly and the sound of soles slapping down the hallway again at a faster pace terrified her.

The door to her room opened and the light flipped on, causing her to blink against the brightness. The man from before, the one who'd spoken to her, entered. He approached with a gun in his hand. She shrank back when she saw it.

"This is not for you. Not yet, anyway. I'm going

to release your legs and you will walk with me. Try anything stupid and I'll kill you." He reached down and unclipped her cuffs from the bar and then released her ankles from it, too. "Get up."

She rolled to her knees and groaned. The damage the asphalt had done to them speared bolts of pain through her legs. She tried to push herself up, but her legs wouldn't hold her.

"I said get up!" The man jerked her into a standing position and her legs crumpled beneath her. She scrambled to get them to obey. She moved forward when he pushed her, swaying like a drunkard, but she kept putting one foot in front of the other.

She leaned into his hold, needing it to keep her upright as blood returned to her legs. The needles of sensation tattooed pain throughout her lower body, but she kept walking. He stopped her at the door and held her as he dumped a pillow from its case. The material went over her head. "You were unconscious when he brought you here. I do not want you to be able to lead them back here."

She trembled at the words. *It sounded as if he was going to free her...* He tugged at her again, and she moved, taking small baby steps until he yanked her. She tried to keep up.

"Stairs."

Her foot scraped along the top ledge and she slid, stumbling down the steps, only kept upright by the force of his grip on her arm. Finally, they reached level ground. It had to be a massive space. Things, like their movement, sounded different, almost like it echoed.

"Get in." She could hear a door open and felt a hand on her head push her down. She shimmied into the car and drew her feet up just as the door slammed shut behind her. She could hear the man walk around the vehicle. He talked to someone and then opened the passenger door. *So, someone else was driving.*

She pushed her feet to the floorboard and hit… *a divider.* It rattled. Like a cage. "Stay down and don't move." Her liberator—or captor—yelled at her. She folded her legs back up and tried to breathe through the mounting fear and almost-crippling anxiety.

The trip didn't take long. She tried to remember the turns, but there were so many stops and starts. The driver used his blinker to turn corners and to change lanes. Very precise because, yeah, who wanted to be pulled over with a bound woman in the back seat?

Gravel. The vehicle was off the blacktop. It moved forward slowly, and then the brakes squealed slightly as they stopped. She heard the driver put the vehicle into park. The door at her feet opened, and she shuffled like an inchworm backward. That's when the pillowcase moved and she could see the floor of the car. She paused for an instant when she recognized the metal cage in the middle of the car. It was a police car or a security vehicle. She wiggled back again and awkwardly found her footing. She dragged her chest against the seat, which moved the pillowcase again. The paint was a dark red. A rush of relief filled her. The patrol cars of HCPD were black and white.

The same vicious hold yanked her upright, twisted her around, and then pushed her forward. She walked on the gravel and felt as the ground got... *spongy*. She took a deep breath through the cotton of the pillowcase. *The harbor.* They were at the harbor. God, were they going to kill her and dump her in the harbor? All they'd have to do is push her overboard. With the ball gag in her mouth and the cuffs binding her hands, she wouldn't be able to tread water for long.

"Lift your foot and step in." She did as he asked,

and he pushed her to the side. She stepped down into... *a boat*. He shoved her in the rest of the way and dropped her onto a seat. She could feel the boat rock as they worked it away from the shore with paddles. The utter silence other than the sounds of the paddles at both sides of the boat was eerie. The harbor was a bustling place. There should be sounds of boats coming and going. She sat quietly for several long moments before she heard the sounds of the harbor.

An inlet or a cove, perhaps? They continued to move for at least ten minutes. Finally, the oars stopped the rhythmic tug and pull through the water. The boat bobbed and scraped against something. She twisted at the sound. "We have three minutes before I'm going to take you up these stairs. You are going to stay plastered to my front. You try to pull away or play dead and you will die. You don't move unless I move you. Understand?" She nodded and prayed he could see the movement under the pillowcase. "That's a good girl. If you behave and your captain is smart and does what I've told him to do, you'll live to see the sunrise. If not, I'll kill you."

If Ryker did what they told him to do... What had he instructed? She closed her eyes behind the material and felt tears streak down her cheeks. Please, God, whatever was going to happen to her would happen, but she prayed for Ryker. Please, don't let tonight scar his soul. He carried so many scars already, loving her shouldn't cause another one. She sniffed, trying to clear her nose.

The man made a disgusted grunt. "All right. Time to move."

Ryker walked down the long pier. The high arc-necked lights that lined the pier brightened a twelve-foot circle before darkness shadowed him. The next light cast its glow, and he walked through it. He'd walked forward, watched as they appeared at the end of the pier. How long had they been waiting? His people had reported no movement.

He continued walking. "Stop there." The same voice was on the phone. "Turn around."

Ryker elevated his one arm and slowly circled. "I want to see her." He stopped, facing the man.

"This is not my doing. She is not worth a war. I want to earn a living, make my bosses happy, and move up."

"I want to see her." The clothes were Brie's, but

he wouldn't put it past these bastards to put another woman under that pillowcase.

The man jerked the material off and he saw red. Blood caked on her face, and her mouth was stretched obscenely by a ball gag. She sagged, and he heard her muffled cry.

"This is what we are going to do. I'm going to walk down these steps. There is a gun on her. My shooter will not fail. You move a muscle, she dies."

"You have a gun on her?" He repeated the words to make sure his people heard them.

"We're on it. Give us some time, Terrell."

Ryker spread his legs shoulder-width apart, his firing stance. "I'm not moving, but I don't get your motivation. What are you gaining by bringing her to me?" He kept his hand in the air, away from his weapon.

"Motivation? There is no motivation other than doing what was going to eventually happen. I saw an opportunity to discredit them with those above, and I took it. I allow her to die and the commissioner of the police force declares war because he's lost a daughter. The mourning lover goes rogue and my distribution is disrupted, or worse, halted. The men who supply the drugs become disgruntled and think maybe my little coup was against the better good. They kill me and then all my groveling under those two was for nothing."

"Eyes on shooter." The words came through his earpiece. "I have a clear shot." The sharpshooter acknowledged his ability to hit the target if required.

"Your play, Ryker." He heard the Commissioner's voice. A shrill ring of a cell phone split the silence.

Without a word, the man stepped backward off the dock, and both he and Brie disappeared from view.

Ryker pulled his weapon and ran to the edge of the dock. A bullet hit the edge as he peeked out. He ducked back and leaned forward, lower. He leveled his gun and shot the man who stood next to Brie on the deck of the speedboat.

The man twisted, losing his footing. He knocked Brie into the water but stayed in the boat as the driver slammed the throttle forward, launching the boat into the harbor.

There was no thought as he plunged into the water off the pier. With his near useless arm pinned to his side, he swam using a one-armed stroke to the place where he'd last seen Brie floundering. Filling his lungs with air, he dove. He could see her hair floating in the water. He grabbed at it, snatching a handful of her beautiful brown hair before he righted and kicked to the surface.

He arched his back and forced her to the surface across his chest. Kicking with his legs, he pushed her up past the surface of the water. Punching the water with his legs, he attempted to pierce the surface and fill his lungs, but he couldn't. Fire-laced steel bands crushed his chest as he fought the urge to exhale.

A flurry of movement beside him removed Brie's weight, giving him the buoyancy to surface. Gasping for air, someone grabbed him from behind. "Stop fighting, damn it, Cap! Brock's got Brie, let me help you to the fucking dock."

"I can swim." He coughed, filled his lungs with air, and rolled from Brody's hold and struck out with his one-armed sidestroke. Brody swam beside him and helped him up onto the water-level landing at the pier. Brock's back as he bent over Brie prevented Ryker from seeing her. He crawled forward on his knees. The ball gag was gone, leaving horrendous impressions on her face, but her eyes were open, and she reached to him.

He grabbed her hand, dropped to his ass beside her, and pulled her to him with his good arm.

Their tears merged with the saltwater from the harbor.

"I'm okay. I'm okay." Her whispered affirmations seemed to be more for herself than for him, but he agreed with each statement and held her as tight as he could. When her words stilled, he rocked with her in his arms, kissing her forehead, unable to release her from the crushing hold, afraid that if he did, she'd disappear. Stupid and juvenile, but damn it, he'd almost lost her in that water. The fear of trying to keep her floating and the certainty that he was going to black out from a lack of oxygen had twisted his guts into a churning mess. Fuck, he was trembling, and damn it, tears still ran down his cheeks.

He whispered how much he loved her, trying to express with words the relief he was feeling having her in his arms. She burrowed closer, just like she did in bed as if she could meld their two bodies into one.

He closed his eyes and drew a steadying breath until he heard the thunderous sound of someone running down the wooden pier. Her father flew down the stairs and was beside them on the wood planking seconds later.

Ryker was unprepared for the massive bear hug

that encompassed not only Brie but him as well. Brie's father said a prayer of thanks that rushed from his lips. He released Brie and her father gathered her in his arms, although Ryker never let go of her hand that she'd given him. He couldn't lose the connection to her. Not yet.

"I could have killed you for diving off that damn pier." He turned at Brody's hoarse whisper, pulling his gaze away from Brie and her father.

"She would have died if he hadn't." Brock coughed and moved, the pool of water under him squelching around his jeans as he moved to lean back against the pier.

"How bad did you fuck up your shoulder?" Brody nodded his direction.

He moved it and winced as a bolt of pain traveled from his neck to his fingertips. "Not too bad." Which was a fucking whale of a lie. He'd righteously screwed it up.

"Right," Brody snorted.

"You boys get going. I've got Brie, and an ambulance is en route. Brock, the SWAT team is coordinating a search for that damn boat, get up there and flag down the ambulance crew, would you?"

Brock nodded and headed up the stairs. Brie

squeezed Ryker's hand. Her terrified gaze went straight to him. "Where are you going?"

Ryker's eyes went to Brie's immediately. "Brody, tell Terrence he has operational control." He turned and brought her hand to his lips. "Nowhere, babe. I'm staying right here."

Brody stood and answered Brie's question, "There's a raid, three buildings that Peña and Rubio used for business."

Brie coughed but held up the hand Ryker wasn't holding, stilling her brother's movements. She finally drew in enough air to ask, "Is one of them a warehouse with a living area above?"

Ryker exchanged looks with Brody before he answered, "Yes."

"That's probably where he's going. It's where he killed those two men. The ones that took me from behind the restaurant."

Ryker glanced at Brody and then met Chauncey's eyes as he asked, "The man that held you at the end of the pier killed them?"

Brie nodded. "I'm pretty sure he did. There were at least ten shots fired, maybe more." She squeezed Ryker's hand. "Go, do your job. I'll be all right. Dad's here and I can't stand the thought of that man being out there." She pushed her wet hair away from her neck. "He's articulate and cunning, but there was no remorse in him. He didn't want a war with the police and was willing to try to stop it, but everything in me told me that man would kill me if I didn't do exactly as he said. He would have no problem with killing me or you or anyone else. None."

Brody extended a hand to Ryker, but he ignored it. He cradled Brie's hand and kissed her palm. "Are you sure?"

She closed her eyes and nodded before she answered, "Call me as soon as you can."

It took everything he had not to let his voice crack. "I will. I love you."

"I know. I love you, too. Go do your job then come home to me." Brody once again offered him a hand up and he took the help, lifting off the wooden pier. He nodded to the Commissioner, who nodded back. Ryker followed Brody up the stairs. It was time to take these bastards down for good.

CHAPTER 18

"You should let them take you to the emergency room," her father's growl of disapproval floated her way once again.

Brie rolled her shoulders. "I didn't drown. Yeah, I swallowed some of that crappy tasting water, but unless I get sick from that, I'm fine." She'd spent the last three hours giving her statement at the end of the pier. Her clothes stank and so did she.

"You whacked your head against the blacktop," her father retorted.

"I did. The paramedic said my eyes were fine—equal and reactive. I have a headache, but I'm sure that's stress-related. I just want to go home, shower, and wait for Ryker."

"Your mom is going to love fussing over you."

Brie snapped her head in her dad's direction. "Ah, no. Not that home. I want to go to *my* home and wait for Ryker."

"You mean Blay's apartment?" Her father's brow creased in confusion.

"Yeah." She needed to talk to Blay to see if he'd be willing to sell his apartment to them. She shrugged off that thought. She should probably wait to talk to Ryker before making major decisions like buying apartments.

"You'll be alone there. You could have a concussion." Her father crossed his arms over his chest.

"How about I call someone to come stay with me until Ryker clears up this... case? Is it a case?" She tipped her chin and looked at her dad. The grey at his sideburns was more pronounced. Bekki and Blay's fault, not hers.

"It is a lot more than a single case. Your man is on the point of one of the largest busts we've had in the history of Hope City." He winked at her. "Damn proud of you for picking one of the best cops on the force to fall in love with."

She melted into a wide smile. "He is a good cop... Oh, Dad. The car that brought me to the harbor—someone other than the guy who talked to Ryker drove it. I think it was a cop because there was a cage in the back like a police vehicle has, the metal sheet that prevents someone from getting to the front seat. The car was burgundy red. At least the portion of the back door I saw was burgundy."

Her father's brow drew into deep creases. "Burgundy?"

"Yeah, weird, huh?"

He looked past her and nodded. "Really weird. Use my phone and make that call for someone to come stay with you."

Brie narrowed her eyes at her father. "Why are you suddenly giving up? Do you know something about that car?"

He chuckled. "No, but I need to be available if I'm needed."

"I'm not buying it." She smiled down at the picture of her mom that her dad kept as his home screen. "I really don't need anyone to stay with me."

Her father put a hand on her arm. "Brie, tonight, you saw one man murdered, you shot someone, you were kidnapped, knocked out, threatened, transported here with a hood on under the threat of death, and nearly drowned. Forgive me if I want someone with you when all of that crashes around you, because it will. Eventually, it will all land and you're going to have to deal with it. I don't want you alone."

"Wow. Okay, hearing it like that..." She drew a breath. Now she was shaking again. Somehow, she hadn't strung all the events together in her mind even after giving her statement. She trembled and wrapped the blanket someone had handed her earlier around her tighter. "Do you think Blay is working?"

"One way to find out." Her dad took the phone from her hand and made the call. "Blay, sorry for calling so early. Are you working today?" Her father glanced at her as he spoke. "No, that would be perfect. I'm going to need you to swing by your apartment. I'll explain it all when you get here. Good. Yep, see you then. Love you, Son." He hung up the phone and pocketed it. "He's just finishing up shift change. We'll catch a ride to the apartment and I'll stay with you until Blay comes by."

"I'm sorry." Tears formed in her eyes, but she had no idea why.

"Ahhh... there it is." Her dad opened his arms. She dove into the enormous chest and powerful arms that had always protected her. "It's okay, sweetie. Let's keep it together for another couple minutes." He rubbed her back and started her walking down the pier.

It took fifteen minutes to get to the apartment, and Blay was standing at the front door. His eyes widened when he saw her and then narrowed, hardening to a cold, frosty glaze. "I'll kill the bastard." Blay ground the words through clenched teeth.

"It wasn't Ryker. Could you get the door, Son?" Brie sniffled as Blay opened the door. They all marched up the stairs together. She heard Blay ask her father what happened, but obviously, her dad gave him a look to shut him up. Blay unlocked all the locks on the apartment. She walked directly to the bathroom, turned on the shower, and stripped. She needed the stench of the harbor off her and she needed warm water. Lots of warm water.

Sitting down in the middle of the shower, she wrapped her arms around her knees to still the violent shaking. The warm water sprayed down on her aching muscles. She lowered her head to her knees and let the fear wash over her with the spray of the shower.

She could have been killed. The realization pulverized her hastily-shored-up emotional defenses. She let the tears flow. Cathartic and cleansing, that's what her mother called these types of cries. Only the fear was still there, just under her skin. It crawled against her nerves sending constant messages to her brain. Panic, anxiety, fear... all of the emotions sat next to her on that tile floor. She could feel them as if they were living beings.

It was stupid to allow them power now. She *knew* she was safe. She wasn't alone, she had Blay and her father here, but how did she turn off what had happened? She quieted her sobbing and rocked a bit, giving herself something else to focus on.

It didn't work. *God, what she'd seen and what she'd imagined, the thoughts that still raced through her brain hadn't quieted in the slightest.* Since her father had strung each event together for her, she'd been replaying the moments in sequence. The totality of the evening overwhelmed her ability to put any of the thoughts into a cohesive perspective. She'd get there eventually, but it would not happen today. Today she was going to let herself feel the emotions that surrounded her. She'd find a way to put things into perspective. But not today.

She tipped back her head and glanced way up to where the shampoo and soap waited for her. Maybe she'd just soak up the warmth for a bit longer.

Blay rubbed his face with his hands. Scrubbed it, rather. *Holy hell. Someone kidnapped Brianna. She'd shot a man. Almost drowned?*

"Are you tracking here, Son?" His dad's question rang loud and clear in the kitchen.

He nodded his head. "Yeah. I'm staying here until either you or Ryker come back."

"You're off for forty-eight?"

He nodded. "Yeah, just finished my seventy-two-hour shift. I've got plenty of time. You go do what you need to do. I'll fix her some breakfast and then tuck her into bed."

"It might be better to ask her to sit with you here and watch television. If she wakes up in a dark room alone..."

Blay bounced his foot as he leaned against the

kitchen counter. "Oh, shit. Didn't think about that. Yeah, okay. I can do that."

"I appreciate it. I'll call your mother on the way to my office. I'm going to make her promise not to leave the house until we have this guy in custody."

"When is the sweep going to happen?"

His father glanced at his watch. "It started twenty-five minutes ago."

Ryker approached the van. The HCPD sweats he wore were dry, but that did little to stop the reek of the harbor, and taking time to shower was out of the question. Thank God he had extra running shoes in his office. He'd eaten some over-the-counter painkillers and downed two cups of coffee. He was hurting and tired, but he'd be damned if he'd step down from the helm of this bust.

He tapped quietly on the back door of the command vehicle disguised as a city utility vehicle. Stepping up into the van, he nodded at the officers already working the comms. He put his headset on. "Command to Team One, status." His voice rang across the radios in the front of the van, squelching a high tone through the system. He covered his mic. "Secure your comms."

Patel yelled at him from the front seat: "Sorry. Okay, they're off, go ahead."

"Command to Team One, status."

"Team One, ready."

"Command to Team Two, status." He waited for the reply and repeated his check on Team Three.

"All Teams, this is Command. Proceed to your Alpha position and check in." He received acknowledgements and watched as his teams drove from the parking lot in armored vehicles.

"Which site, sir?"

He sat down and buckled in. "Position us at Alpha point with Team Two."

Peña and Rubio were deadly, but they liked the comfort that their money could buy. His bet was they'd been nesting inside the warehouse, and that was where they'd fled when Brie had shot Peña. Sarah said the apartment was opulent—or in her words, the place was 'lit'—and they kept most of the drugs on the premises.

Which raised an interesting question. Why would they keep their stock readily available, loaded in trucks so they could move their inventory at a moment's notice? Why wouldn't they cut it and distribute it immediately? Unless the fuckers were operating the logistical branch of the business right under HCPD's nose.

He shook his head and held on as Patel maneuvered the command van into traffic. The cartel's time in Hope City was dwindling. Ryker shifted and eased his shoulder. He wanted to be at the tip of the spear with his team, but he was fucking sidelined *and* hurting. Regardless, they were striking a major blow this morning. He said a quick prayer for those taking part in the sweep.

When Patel turned into the parking lot with Team Two, his people went into a flurry of activity. They activated the video feeds and checked radio communications. He dismounted the van and made his way through a gauntlet of personnel making final adjustments to uniforms and checking weapons and comms.

He edged Tiernan away from the crowd. "Your people know what to expect?"

Tiernan nodded. "We are going in expecting hostilities. It is our normal play, and we'll exercise extreme diligence."

"Be careful and don't get dead." Ryker extended his hand to his friend.

"That's always the plan, my man." Tiernan

shook his hand and nodded to the command vehicle. "You're not taking a position, right?"

"No. Not unless hell freezes over." He eased his
shoulder again. "I think I'll take it easy today."

Tiernan snorted, "Right."

He laughed and headed back to the command
vehicle. When he put on the headphones and
adjusted his monitor, it was time to move his
people into harm's way.

Ryker cleared his throat. "Listen up. Each of
you focuses on your team. I'll be on all frequencies.
If you need a wide broadcast, relay it to me." He
ran down the checklist. "Helmet cams."

"Team One, good feed."

"Team Two, good feed."

"Team Three, good feed."

He nodded and did the same for comms and his
team echoed the same responses. It was redundant,
but one malfunctioning piece of equipment could
cost lives. Ryker looked up when the timer activated. He keyed his mic and issued the alert. "Team
One, Two, and Three, two-minute warning."

He heard the doors closing on the two assault
vehicles next to the command van. The engines
cranked and all three team leads acknowledged his
warning.

He watched the clock as the digital display counted down. At exactly zero six hundred, he keyed his mic. "All teams, go."

As expected, Team Three hit their building first. Patel logged the exact time of arrival as did his other people when teams One and Two arrived on scene. "All teams on scene. Deploy." At his words, the body armor and helmet cams moved, and they watched in real-time as the teams advanced on the sites.

SWAT breached the buildings and a coordinated mayhem ensued. Each team worked to clear their facilities. They expected several non-hostile personnel at Lieutenant Theron's site. King's SWAT Team moved in with spotlights, speakers, and flashbangs. The plan for the hit squad's confusion at the breach worked like a charm. Video screens showed handcuffed personnel being escorted from the scene, but his focus stayed on Team Two. The SWAT teams worked methodically to clear the downstairs area of the warehouse as quietly as possible. This was a stealth takedown, not a quick strike. Whispered check-ins cleared the area as they moved toward the stairs.

A gunshot rang through the comms. The noise froze every one of his teammates in the control vehicle and all eyes pinned to the monitor. "Shots fired! Squad Two, take overwatch." Tiernan's voice confirmed what they already knew and set his people into action.

Ryker switched his comms to speak to his JDET team outside the warehouse. "Shots fired inside. Keep your eyes peeled." They acknowledged his command, and he flipped his mic off. There were seven different exits to that building.

"We have runners. East side of the building."

"Shots fired. Officer down!"

One of his newer team members called in, "Shit, Dobson's hit. I need backup!"

Ryker hit his mic. "Markel and Faison, back up O'Shay." He turned to Patel. "Get an ambulance back there as soon as that area is clear of hostiles."

O'Shay's voice panted across the radio, "Cap, they're heading west. They're in the alley. Two males, black pants, white shirts, both armed. We have three stopped here."

Ryker tossed his headset to Patel. "Get that BOLO out to patrols holding the outer cordon."

Patel caught the headset with one hand but yelled, "Cap, wait!"

He spun at her call. She handed him a portable

radio. "In case you need backup." She put on the headset and sat down.

Ryker clipped the radio onto his waistband and sprinted to the east to intercept the men running west. He removed his arm from its sling as he ran, tossing the damn thing. He slowed to a jog and yanked his radio from his pocket, keeping the volume down as he listened to Patel lead the response. He slowed to a walk. There were two avenues of escape for the perps. They could take Friarwood Drive, which would expose them to any responding patrols, or they could keep to the alley-ways. Ryker carefully moved to the path he'd take to avoid being seen. He slid into the alley and worked his way up about halfway, taking cover by an overflowing dumpster. His best chance to take down two perps without killing anyone, himself included, was the element of surprise. He moved a box in front of him as he heard the distinct sound of someone running on the pavement to his east.

He flexed his hand and extended his bad arm as best as possible as he waited. It was either one person, or the perps' steps were in unison. He waited, hidden as they jogged past. Black slacks, white shirts. Ryker stood and pointed his weapon at the men. "Freeze! Police!"

The men skidded to a halt. "Put your hands up where I can see them." He made his way through the rubble that had concealed him. "Higher. You on the right, drop to your knees."

The man on the right dropped to his knees. "You on the left, walk forward five steps." He couldn't call in backup until they were both under control. As the other man walked forward, he used his cuffs to snag one of the other man's wrists and had him on his stomach, cuffed in less than ten seconds.

Ryker approached the other man. "You don't think I'm going to allow you to cuff me, do you, Captain Terrel?" The man clasped his hands behind his head and turned around. Ryker held his service weapon on the man who'd thrown Brie into the water not more than four hours ago.

"I think you're going to do exactly that." Ryker motioned to the ground. "Get on your knees."

The man smiled, an inappropriate action that sent a shrill siren of warning through him. The man was too confident.

"I will kneel for no one." The man shrugged with his hands still behind his head. "How is your shoulder, Captain?"

Ryker could see the perp he'd cuffed in his

peripheral vision. He'd rolled to his side, but the man wasn't going anywhere. There was something off. His gut was screaming at him to be cautious, but he needed this man cuffed before he called in backup. "On. Your. Knees." He held his gun on the man.

"Ah, Captain... I know you won't shoot me for not going to my knees." The man shifted his legs. Ryker recognized the fighting stance immediately.

The move was sudden and deadly. A throwing star catapulted in his direction. Only years of training in the martial arts prevented the weapon from being buried in his flesh. The moment it took to move gave the perp his opportunity, and the man came at him with caged fury. His gun was kicked from his hand and it skittered across the asphalt. Ryker dropped and swept with his leg, surprising the bastard. He caught the ankle, and the man went down, but they both popped up in fighting stances.

The man's eyes lit up, and he smiled again. He taunted, "Oh, yes, I do so enjoy a good fight."

Ryker's arm was screaming like a bitch. He protected it and held it against his stomach. He'd beat this motherfucker with one arm. There was no other option.

He dropped back, baiting the bastard. He feigned a backward step when the man approached. Ryker blocked a punch with his good arm and ducked a follow up right hook. Instinctively, he flattened his hand and used the curve between his thumb and pointer finger to throat punch. The fucker retreated and narrowed his eyes before he snarled and approached again. Ryker ducked the left cross and slammed a driving punch with his good hand into the bastard's ribs.

The man gasped as he dropped back. His eyes narrowed as a feral snarl curled his lip before he moved forward again. Ryker bounced on his toes, keeping his bad arm pinned to his stomach. The bastard might have had a throwing star, but he wasn't well trained. Ryker sneered at the bastard and returned the taunt. "I love a good fight, too." He bolted forward and elevated his good arm high over the man's head, bringing the other man's arms up to block a blow that would never come. He kicked the bastard's knee. The joint popped, and he went down partway.

The perp snapped forward, sending his arm in an arc. His fist landed on Ryker's injured shoulder. Black spots ravaged his vision and his knees gave out. He went down like a fucking rock. The bastard came at him, his rage pinpointed on Ryker's neck, and the perp locked both hands around it.

His reflex actions from countless hours on the training mat kicked in. Ryker bridged his back, trapped the man's arms with his good arm, slipped his foot to the outside of the man's leg, and flipped them both to the side. He rolled them, and with every ounce of strength he had left, he threw a left hook. The guy went limp and Ryker sat back on his heels.

The fucker was still breathing. *Thank God.* He stared at the man's face. Other than seeing him tonight with Brie, he'd never seen the man before. Was he a major player in the Cartel? Had he killed Peña and Rubio? Was he the top of the organization now? So many fucking questions and not a single answer. Yet.

Black spots still danced in front of his eyes. He blinked them clear and groaned as he stood up. He stared at the man he'd cuffed earlier. The guy wasn't even trying to move. *Smart man.* He bent and picked up his weapon and then looked for his radio. Damn it, where had it gone?

A rush of feet breached the mouth of the alley.

Uniformed officers leveled their weapons and screamed for him to drop his weapon.

Ryker hung his head and stared at the word POLICE emblazoned down his leg and across his chest of his sweats. *Stupid.* No, not really. The cop was being cautious, which was good. He carefully lowered the weapon to the ground and backed away from it as directed. He didn't want to get shot *again,* and not following the directions a cop gave you upped that probability.

"Arms up! Get on your knees!"

Ryker snorted. Yeah, where had he heard that before? He obliged with his left arm. "My right arm is broken. I'm Captain Ryker Terrell, HCPD JDET. These two are the runners from the warehouse sweep. Call it in and ask."

"I'll do that once you go to your knees." The cop moved up and kicked his weapon away.

"Dude, that is my service weapon. If you fuck it up, I'm having the department come after you for the cost of repair." Ryker dropped to his knees and then sat on his heels. Man, he'd seriously fucked up the doc's work on his shoulder.

He heard the uniform call it in and heard Patel's voice answer. He sniggered when she cussed over the radio. She was a momma bear.

One of the uniforms brought his weapon and handed it to him as the other cuffed the man who'd dropped Brie into the harbor. "Did he break your arm, sir?"

"No. I had shoulder replacement surgery about a week ago."

"Holy hell, you took down two perps one-armed?"

"Yeah, and I thought you were going to take it easy today." Tiernan's smart ass comment brought a smile to his face, but he wasn't moving. Actually, he couldn't. If he did, he'd puke. He was done.

Tiernan crouched down beside him. "Dobson?" Ryker needed an update on the hurt member of his team.

"He'll live. Not sure if he'll be back to work anytime soon. Looks like the bullet went through his ankle."

"I can recommend a doctor." Ryker tried to lose the exhaustion, but damn it, he was fucking tired. "The op?"

"From what I'm getting from Control, we have all three sites secured. No casualties. My guys took down three in the warehouse, but we were able to get medical to them in time. They opened fire on us. We have it on video for internal affairs. How about we get you to the hospital?"

Ryker nodded. "Yeah, that would probably be good."

"Fucker nailed you in the shoulder, didn't he?" Tiernan offered him a hand up.

"Yeah. Do me a favor, would yah? Find out who the hell that guy is and make sure they watch him close. He's mental."

Tiernan chuckled as he ducked under Ryker's good arm. Ryker groaned but appreciated the support. "He's not the only one who's mental. You'd probably give him a run for his money."

"Not funny."

Tiernan laughed and started them toward the mouth of the alley. "Yeah, it really is."

Ryker focused on moving one foot in front of the other. Okay, it probably was fucking hilarious. He'd laugh tomorrow.

Maybe.

CHAPTER 19

R yker opened his eyes. *Fuck. Right, the hospital. Again.*

"Hi." Brie leaned over him.

"Babe." The word sounded like a croaking toad with a mouth full of flies, but she smiled at him. Fuck, he'd never get enough of that smile.

"The doctor was pretty upset with you." She pushed the hair off his forehead.

"Not my fault." He blinked up at her. "How are you?"

Her smile faltered for a moment. "Scared. Tired. Sore."

He lifted his head and glanced down at the bed. He didn't have an IV stuck in him, so he tapped the silver rail with his hand. "Put this down and lie down with me."

She shook her head. "I don't want to hurt you."

"The only thing that is going to hurt me is you not getting in this bed and holding me." He tapped the bar again.

Brie glanced at the door. "I'll get in trouble."

"No. Come on. I'll protect you from the mean nurses."

She chuckled and shook her head. "You couldn't protect me from a two-day-old kitten right now."

"Okay, then you come protect me from the mean nurses. Please, babe, I need to hold you." Ryker reached up and touched the bruise on her face. "I need to know you're okay."

Brie glanced at the door again before she hit the button to lower the rail. He brought up his good arm, and she snuggled in beside him. Her leg over his, her head on his good shoulder, and her arm folded across his abdomen. Her warmth immediately wrapped around him. He kissed the top of her head. "Tell me what you're afraid of."

She puffed a small exhale of air. "I don't know. I guess my sense of safety is shaky. I mean, when those guys were harassing me, I still had a bit of control, you know? Then those other guys showed up and... I can still see Blondie hitting the wall and then... that man put a bullet in his head."

Ryker closed his eyes for a moment, trying hard to find a calm place that he could talk from, but... "Someone was harassing you? Who is Blondie?"

Her body tensed for a moment. "Blondie is what I called the guy. He was the one that sliced my tire. He and his friend kept turning up to hassle me. I don't really know why. I thought the harassment was tied to the pressure Councilman Davis has been putting on me to pay him to get my agenda item about donating food to the homeless shelter in front of the city council."

His hand stilled on her hair. "I don't believe we talked about any of those issues."

She shook her head and looked up at him. "No, I was trying to take care of it by myself."

He kissed her forehead. "Why were you hesitant to tell me?"

She sighed and snuggled closer under his chin. "I don't know. I was afraid of bothering you, of depending on someone else, and yeah, maybe I didn't want you to march in and tell me what I should do."

He closed his eyes and started stroking her long

brown hair again. "We need to work on our communication, or our marriage is going to be rocky."

She tipped her head back again. "Did you just ask me to marry you?"

He opened his eyes and smiled at her. "No. I'm not giving you a chance to say no."

She smiled and kissed his chin. "Then I say yes." She yawned and snuggled nearer to him again. He held her against him and let himself drift to sleep.

The light from the hall woke him. Brody stood in the doorway, glowering at the bed. Ryker shifted and then realized Brie was still sleeping with him. He wrapped his good arm around her and motioned with his fingers for Brody to come in.

His sergeant pulled up a chair near the head of the bed on the opposite side of his sister.

"Sit rep?" Ryker whispered the words.

Brody leaned forward and spoke quietly. "The guy you took down in the alley is Gary Cava. He's a big man on the West Coast. The feds are all over him. Seems he's been expanding by taking out regional kingpins. He's a conduit for the feds to reach the cartel leadership. He admitted to killing Peña and Rubio. The fucker knows he's going to get a deal from the feds to testify. He's a straight-up killer, Cap. He could have put a bullet in Brie at any time, but according to the feds I talked to, he has a strange moral code. He skinned one of his top lieutenants alive for killing a kid's dog and then he bought the kid a new puppy. She's fucking lucky to be here." Brody's voice cracked.

Ryker could feel his eyes filling. He closed them and tightened his arm around her. She squirmed a bit and he loosened his hold. "Go on." He blinked his eyes open.

"We let Mouse know she was safe. The doctor wasn't happy about the drive-by, but the lieutenant felt it would help her get better, and she risked it all to talk to us, so he drove to New York after we knew you would be okay."

"Bet Fenton had a field day with that." Ryker rolled his eyes. *Fenton, what a douche.*

"Well, I have some intel on that issue, but no one knows this yet." Ryker lifted an eyebrow. "Seems Colonel Fenton is retiring. He hasn't been given an option. The videos that were taken in the squad room when he was ranting and raving made it to the internet. They went viral and the mayor's office acted."

"Well, I'll be damned." He moved slightly and

winced. His body had been used up. He wasn't being a baby by admitting he was damn sore.

"Probably, but that's not my doing." Brody chuckled a bit and so did Ryker. Brody sighed. "We found the vehicle Rubio and Peña used for the drive-by on your house at the warehouse. We got one of the hit squad to roll for a promise of WitSec. The feds agreed. The guy confirmed they did the drive-by because you had access to Mouse. The woman had seen too much, they wanted her dead, and they were sending a message."

"Hell of a message. Idiots. Did they actually think we'd give them Mouse?"

Brody shrugged. "Delusions of grandeur and all that shit. Untouchable. They thought they were untouchable." Ryker nodded in agreement. "There are a couple loose ends. Brie said the car she was transported in had a police cage in the back and was burgundy in color."

Ryker turned his head and stared at his officer. "An unmarked car?"

"We had that thought, too." Brody pulled a piece of paper out of his pocket. "Six burgundy unmarked in the fleet. Two were in for maintenance. The rest were accounted for. Mozinga and Dawson are looking into who had access to the two vehicles in the maintenance yard, but it is looking like a dead end."

Ryker nodded. He lightly ran his hand up and down Brie's arm. "So, it's over. For her." He spoke to himself, but Brody answered.

"Yeah, except for that dickwad councilman. But Bekki is on that shit like stink on week-old garbage. She's going to take that bastard down. I can hardly wait."

Ryker shifted and asked, "Shouldn't there be criminal charges?"

"Yeah, but there is nothing but hearsay now, and we don't know that the guys in the alleyway that were harassing Brie were connected to the councilman. Nothing to tie them to the guy. Let Bekki ferret out the rest of the rats and then the police can get involved."

"I guess we'll have to do that."

"And you're off for the next four weeks. Deputy Commissioner Duckworth has sent word to the team that if she finds out you're working we'll lose *our* positions. So, you're persona non grata."

Ryker chuckled. "I can live with that."

Brody stood. "Good, because I like my job. Besides, you two need to mend." He nodded to his sister. "Take care of her, Cap." Brody placed the chair back and headed to the door. He stopped and smiled at his sister. "I'm glad for both of you."

Ryker watched the door swing shut and closed his eyes, holding the woman he loved. Maybe this time he was enough. God, he prayed he would never let this woman down.

"It's a freaking disaster." Brie glanced at the vehicles parked outside of the huge house.

"It's just your family." *Maybe.* There were several cars he didn't recognize.

"I told them something small." She parked in the only open slot in front of the house.

"Small for your family is something just this side of five hundred people. You should have been specific with your mom." Hannah King would take the reins in any situation. The woman was full tilt. Always.

"I was! I said small. In what world is all of this small?" Brie spread her arms, indicating the slew of vehicles piled into the cul-de-sac.

"In your mom's world, babe." Ryker chuckled and got out of the passenger side of Brie's vehicle. He'd been damn good about following the doctor's orders this time. He had one more week of medical leave and other than doing some computer work and making sure Terrence and Brody were on track, he'd kept his ass at home, away from any temptation of going back to work too early.

"I'm sorry." She walked up beside him. "I never should have told her we were getting married."

"Like she wouldn't have figured it out when you showed up wearing this ring?" Ryker held her left hand in his. He'd bought her a diamond solitaire. It wasn't huge, he wasn't made of money, but Brie had loved it when they went shopping for rings and that was all that mattered.

"Right? Well, I guess we deal with whatever Mom has in store, huh?"

"Her intentions are good." They held hands as they walked past the cars that lined the street.

Brie stopped and looked at a rather expensive-looking Land Rover parked next to a huge 4x4 truck. "Remember you said that, okay?"

Ryker looked at the vehicles. "Why? Who do these belong to?"

"Us."

Ryker spun. Xander and Killian were on the sidewalk just this side of the gate where the others gathered. "We didn't go in. When we got the call there was going to be an engagement party..." Killian shrugged. "If you don't want us here, we'll call the others and tell them not to come. They are waiting around the corner. We didn't want to ambush you."

Ryker squeezed Brie's hand and held it tight as he approached his brothers. "I'm happy you're here. What will Benjamin say? I'm sure he's against any reconciliation between us."

Xander shrugged. "I've lost a great amount of respect for him, but he is my father. I will always try to be the man he raised me to be. Except in this situation, he is dead wrong, and we've all talked. We're successful. If Father wants to cut ties, we'll all be okay. We hope it won't come to that, but he's hurt all of us by driving a wedge between us. It's time to heal. If he can't be a part of that, it's his own fault."

"Call the rest of the boys then. I'd like you to meet our family." Ryker put his arm around Brie.

"Perfect." Xander smiled as Killian removed his phone from his pocket. He nodded to the sling. "I thought you were supposed to be out of that by now."

Brie tipped back her head and laughed. "Oh,

boy! Xander, why don't we go into the backyard and grab a beer?"

Xander offered her his arm. "Why do I get the feeling there is a story there?"

Ryker watched them walk into the backyard arm-in-arm. "They're on their way." Killian pocketed his phone. "Elias doesn't have much time away from the hospital, but he wanted to be here to congratulate you. Dimitri, Xander, and I can stay for the duration, but we've all agreed if it becomes uncomfortable for you, we'll leave. We don't want to disrupt your life."

Ryker nodded toward the backyard. "That family is like the family we could have been. They are the salt of the earth and are way too deep in each other's business." He turned at the sound of car doors closing. His brothers strode up the walk. They'd changed so much yet remained the same.

Elias was in the lead. Dimitri's smile lit up the street and he bounded forward. The hug wasn't as hard as he was suspecting, which was a godsend. He didn't want to face Doctor Phillips anytime soon. "I missed you, Ry."

He hugged his brother back. "I missed you, too."

Elias hugged him gently after Dimitri moved away. His youngest brother backed away and looked down at his scrubs. "Not really in party attire. I've got to head back. Another resident is covering for me. Killian and Xander will take Dimitri home, but I wanted to come and say congratulations."

"Would you like to meet Brie?" Ryker motioned toward the back yard.

"I really can't today. But next time I get a break, maybe we could do dinner or something?" Elias cautiously offered the suggestion as if Ryker would bat it away like a foul-smelling fish.

Ryker smiled. "We'd like that."

"Yeah?" Elias' smile rivaled Dimitri's.

"Definitely. You name the date, and dinner is on me."

"Thank God. Medical residents do not make a lot of money." Elias gave him another hug. "See you soon." He turned and jogged back to the car they drove up in.

Ryker motioned to his two brothers. "Time to meet the rest of the family."

Brie sat in one of the Adirondack chairs under the weave of fairy lights that her mother loved so much. The day had been long but perfect. Ryker and his brothers had learned to relax around each other as the day wore on. The laughter from the picnic tables where the men gathered brought a smile to her face.

"Goodness, Brie, you didn't find one fantastic man, you found four!" Tara sat down on the lawn with her glass of wine.

"Five. He has four brothers. The youngest is a medical resident and couldn't get away."

"A doctor?" Bekki claimed an empty chair. "Yummy. So, the Terrell brothers are smart *and* good looking."

"Not Terrell, their last name is Ganas. They're half-brothers."

Bekki choked and wine tipped from her glass as she coughed. Brie leaned and whapped her sister on the back. Erin McBride grabbed Brie's arm and stopped her. "You're going to kill her before she catches her breath."

Bekki nodded, still coughing but holding her hand up to stop Brie from pounding her on the back again.

"What's going on?" Caitlyn McBride dropped into another chair.

"Brie is trying to kill Bekki," Erin explained. "Where are the rest of the chicks?"

"Oh. Brie, stop trying to kill Bekki." Caitlyn waved at the house. "Kallie and Amber are keeping the moms and kids occupied in the kitchen while they visit with Kimberly. She's nice and digs the moms. Hey, do you know if any of Ryker's brothers are married?"

"I don't think so. Why? Which one are you targeting?" Brie spoke as she watched Bekki wipe her eyes.

"All of them." Caitlyn and Erin said at the same time. She pointed across the lawn. "Is that Dimitri? He's been talking to Dawn for almost an hour now."

"Reeeaaaallly..." Tara drew out the word. "That should upset the scales."

"What? What are you talking about?" Brie leaned forward and looked around the bush that hid the table where Dawn and Dimitri were sitting.

"You really haven't been around lately, have you? Blay and Dawn are like two magnets that are trying way too hard not to get together if you ask my opinion."

"Blay?" Brie laughed. "No way. Blay is a player. They probably are discussing schedules. Blay sometimes picks up Gage and watches him when he's not working." She shook her head. "I saw Blay the other day, and he was heading to the Celtic Cock to meet some woman from work. You're way off base."

Tara took a drink of her wine and sighed. "I think those two would be fantastic together."

"Stop. You sound like the moms," Caitlyn groaned. "Please don't turn into a matchmaker. You remember how much you hated it, right?"

Brie raised her hand. "I hated it *and* I found someone without my mother's help, thank you very much."

"Speaking of Ryker, when are you getting married?" Bekki croaked the question, still coughing a bit.

"This spring. I want to get married here in the backyard when all the flowers are blooming."

"Oh, man, the moms are going to freak. I can see it now. Our get-togethers will be scheduled around making centerpieces and flowery shit." Erin rolled her eyes.

"As long as I can drink, I can work a glue gun." Brie held up her almost-empty glass. "Thank you in advance for the slightly lopsided centerpieces, the fact that you'll all have to find and wear dresses in shades of yellow, and deal with Hover Mother and her sidekick, Glarin' Sharon."

They all raised their glasses in unison. Brie took a sip and glanced at her watch as Ryker's brothers stood. He motioned for her to join him and she smiled. They'd say goodbye to the brothers and then she was going to take her man home and make love to him. Now that his arm was gaining strength, the nights were becoming more... animated.

Tara leaned into her and whispered, "I know what that smile means."

Brie glanced at her friend. "Did I hear grandma has Colleen tonight?"

"Oh, yeah." Tara wiggled her eyebrows. "Should we go snag our men?"

Brie stood and offered her friend a hand up. "Let's go."

Brie smoothed her brush through her hair and stood back away from the mirror. The new lavender camisole and boy shorts were nothing but lace. She smiled at the way they fit. A small dab of expensive perfume on her wrists and she was ready to play a little game with her man. She was probably going to make a damn fool of herself, but whatever.

She called through the door, "Ryker?"

"Yeah, babe?"

She drew a breath and pushed down the nerves. "What are you doing?"

"Laying down. Do you need something?"

"Yeah, would you come here for a moment?"

She grabbed her phone and connected it to the wireless speaker in the bedroom. She pushed play and opened the door. At the first beat of *Mother Freedom*, she started dancing.

Ryker froze, standing gloriously naked beside the bed. His eyes widened and his mouth opened. She'd taken dance lessons when she was little and more recently pole dancing classes at her gym. It was so easy to sexualize the moves she remembered. She weaved closer to him and shimmied away when he reached for her, his shell-shocked expression still very much in place.

With each drop of bass she unfastened one of the small hooks in the front of her camisole. Ryker finally blinked and sat down on the bed. She smiled and moved forward. She'd never seen a lap dance, but...

"Holy fuck." Ryker's hands fell on her hips as she straddled him and gyrated against him, keeping her moves in beat with the music. She held his hands to her hips and bent backward. He tightened his grip, which was exactly what she needed. She stretched her arms above her head and arched back while sitting on his lap. Her hips kept beat with the song. She straightened and popped the last two hooks holding her cami together. The lace split open.

Ryker's hands rounded to her ass, and he moved her closer. The dance and the music faded into oblivion when his lips found her breast. He laid back on the bed, bringing her with him. He feasted on her breasts, pushing electrified shards of sensation to her core. Their hips moved in perfect harmony, building the tingling thrum just under her skin. He released her tender nipple, and she moved away from him. She ran her hand across his healed incision, then down his chest. She reached behind her and stroked his very hard cock.

Rising to her knees, she let her fingers trail across

the lace of her panties. Ryker's eyes followed her movements. She reached between her legs and released the two tiny snaps securing the lace together. She knew the moment Ryker saw her Brazilian wax. He arched, and she was on her back. He dropped to his knees on the floor and with his good arm tugged her to the edge of the bed. Tongue, lips, teeth, and his five o'clock shadow created delicious friction against her freshly bared skin. She tried to buck against his mouth. God, she needed... more.

"I've got you, babe."

She'd said that out loud? Ryker entered her, one knee on the bed beside her hip, the other leg leveraged against the floor. He bent her leg toward her shoulder, and she gasped as he groaned. She called his name and begged for more. Her finish came fast and hard. She shouted his name and held onto him as he orgasmed right after her.

"Holy hell, woman. Are you trying to kill me?" His words muffled in her hair where he'd dropped after he'd finished.

She panted. "That was good, huh?"

He jacked up his head. Her hair stuck to his face. "That was better than good. When... how... dancing? You're going to kill me." He dropped back down onto the bed.

"So, I take it you don't want me to do that again?" She shrieked when he jolted up suddenly.

"No, you need to do that again. Fuck, it was so hot I wanted to devour you."

"I think you accomplished that." She laughed and he waggled his eyebrows at her.

Suddenly serious, he bent down and kissed her. "You are the most amazing gift. I love you."

She cupped his cheek with her hand. "You are my life." She felt the weight of her love for him settle around her. They were two halves of a whole.

He lowered for another kiss and she fell into the man who'd awakened her soul and saved her life. Her protector, her lover, her friend... her world.

EPILOGUE

Bekki King watched her sister Brie and her fiancé say goodbye to Ryker's brothers. Half-brothers. Which was a major problem. Killian Ganas was a name she knew well. The man's corporation had won a slew of city contracts. According to some, too many.

Caitlyn and Erin stayed silent until Brie and Tara were out of earshot. "Care to tell me what that look is for?" Caitlyn nudged her.

"What look?" She still had her eyes pegged on Killian Ganas. The man was a walking wet dream. Tall, sexy, built, and until just a few moments ago, completely doable.

"I've known you my entire life. I know when

you're up to something. What did Brie say that made you choke on your wine?"

Erin ran her finger around the rim of her wine-glass. "I heard that. She told Bekki that their last name isn't Terrell, it's Ganas." Erin chuckled. "That's when she inhaled her wine and Brie started caving in her spine."

"Do you know him?" Caitlyn leaned to watch the men leave.

"I know *of* him." Bekki leaned back in her chair as Brie and Ryker said their goodbyes.

Erin stared at her and cocked her head. "*Of* him? What does that mean?"

"He's been mentioned by a couple people during the background research for a story I'm working on."

Caitlyn leaned back and stared at her. "That doesn't sound good."

Bekki waved off the concern. "It doesn't sound like anything. Until I find out facts, mentions and rumors are just that. How many times have I gone into a story thinking it would turn out one way and have it hook radically and lead me into a different direction?" Except Killian Ganas was the different direction her story had taken. Damn it.

Caitlyn sniggered. "I don't know... all of them?"

"Exactly. I choked because I recognized the name. You know the Ganas family is loaded. Like, really loaded. Right?"

"Why does that matter?" Erin got up. "Rich does not make a person good."

And wasn't that the truth of the day? "True, just a point of conversation." Bekki stood too. "I better head home. I have several appointments first thing in the morning and I need my beauty sleep."

Caitlyn held up a hand and Bekki braced to pull her up off the grass. Erin was halfway across the lawn when Caitlyn spoke. "You can't fool me. You're going after that guy, as in an investigation, aren't you?"

Bekki nodded her head. "I am. I'm going after him with everything I can muster."

"That won't bode well for family relations."

"Neither does being a crook."

Caitlyn sighed. "Well, there is that."

Would you like to read more? Click here for Killian and Brie's story and here for Rory McBride's story!

Passages: The Kings of Guardian Book 13

A Backwater Blessing: A Kings of Guardian and Heart's Desire Crossover Novella

Montana Guardian: A Kings of Guardian Novella

Guardian Defenders Series

Gabriel

Maliki

Guardian Security Shadow World

Anubis (Guardian Shadow World Book 1)

Asp (Guardian Shadow World Book 2)

Lycos (Guardian Shadow World Book 3)

Thanatos (Guardian Shadow World Book 4)

Tempest (Guardian Shadow World Book 5)

Smoke (Guardian Shadow World Book 6)

STAND ALONE NOVELS

SEAL Forever - Silver SEALs

A Heart's Desire - Stand Alone

Hot SEAL, Single Malt (SEALs in Paradise)

Hot SEAL, Savannah Nights (SEALs in Paradise)

ABOUT THE AUTHOR

USA Today and Amazon Bestselling Author, Kris Michaels is the alter ego of a happily married wife and mother. She writes romance, usually with characters from military and law enforcement backgrounds.

Made in United States
Troutdale, OR
10/04/2023

13415862R00189